WOMEN'S SUFFRAGE

WOMEN'S SUFFRAGE

ISSUE 20

MINERVA RISING PRESS

Tampa

Minerva Rising Press LLC, Tampa
www.minervarising.com

Staff
Kimberly Brown, Executive Editor
Rebecca Beardsall, Creative Nonfiction Editor
Alissa DeLaFuente, Fiction Editor
Emily Lake Hansen, Poetry Editor
Jessica Ciosek, Fiction Reader
Carol Roan, Nonfiction Reader
Natasha Oliver, Fiction Reader
Brooke Schultz, Graphic Designer

ISBN 978-950811-10-6

Minerva Rising is an independent literary journal celebrating the creativity and wisdom in every woman.
We publish thought-provoking fiction, creative nonfiction, essays and poetry, as well as original prints,
photography and graphic art by women writers and artists. Subscriptions are $32 US for one year (three
issues). Minerva Rising accepts unsolicited manuscripts and artwork that address our current theme.
Please visit our website at www.minervarising.com for detailed information on the theme for our next
issue and our submission guidelines.

Contents

Letter from the Editor

I have a framed picture on the wall above our loveseat in my living room – an art piece by Angie Dennis. The print, titled Deeds Not Words, was a gift from my stepson and daughter-in-law in Aotearoa New Zealand. One bird and two women take up prominent space in the art piece.

The bird, the petite and chubby pīwakawaka (fantail), is my favorite Aotearoa New Zealand bird. The first time I saw a little pīwakawaka showing off its beautiful tail was on a visit to my in-laws in Taumarunui. It was love at first sight. I was constantly on the lookout for this cheerful, chatty bird whenever I left the city center where Geoff and I lived. Only years later, I learned the role the pīwakawaka played in the story and death of Maui. Maui was the demigod of Māori and Polynesian myths and legends. There are many stories of Maui doing incredible feats to benefit humans. He fished Aotearoa/New Zealand out of the sea. He captured the sun and beat it into submission to slow down so that humankind could have more time in a day. Maui's last quest was to conquer death and provide immortality to humans. The goddess of the night and death Hine-nui-te-pō ruled the underworld. In order to gain immortality, Maui needed to journey through the vagina of the goddess Hine-nui-te-pō and exit through her mouth. His bird friends warned him of the dangers of such a journey, to which Maui replied, "If you laugh, I will indeed be killed. But if I pass right through her body, I will live, and she will die."

As Maui wiggled into the vagina of Hine-nui-te-pō, the pīwakawaka began to laugh, waking the goddess who crushed Maui with her vagina's obsidian teeth. This was the first vagina dentata story I ever heard. Yes, I realize the story means that death is still a part of life. Yet, I see the pīwakawaka as a feminist ally warning the goddess of the man trying to take her life, her power away from her. I always knew there was a reason I had an instant connection with the pīwakawaka.

The print also contains the likeness of two women on two teacups. The women are Kate Sheppard and Meri Mangakahia, two suffragettes. Both were instrumental in Aotearoa New Zealand becoming the first country in the world where women won the right to vote in 1893. The title of the print, "Deeds Not Words, comes from a famous saying of the UK suffragette Emmeline Pankhurst. Kate Sheppard born in England, emigrated to Aotearoa New Zealand in 1868. She supported and promoted women's suffrage with petitions, meetings, and letter-writing campaigns. Sheppard was the editor of The White Ribbon, the first woman-operated newspaper in Aotearoa New Zealand. Meri Mangakahia born in the Hokianga district was a member of the Te Rarawa iwi. She was of Ngāti Te Rēinga, Ngāti Manawa, and Te Kaitu-tae origin. She was the first woman known to have addressed the parliament on her motion that women participate in selecting members. In her speech, she not only stated that women should be allowed to vote, but that they should also be sitting members of the Māori parliament. Mangakahia argued that Māori women were landowners in their own right and were entitled to have their say in decisions affecting them.

It is impossible for me to go throughout my day without being reminded of the strength of these women and the role they played in changing history. I purposefully decided to hang the picture in my living room, the central place of my home, to honor women and feminism. I was a late-blooming feminist, and my time in Aotearoa New Zealand was the start of it all for me. I would not be where I am today without my transnational identity spanning the United States of America and Aotearoa New Zealand, and without the strength and courage of the women in both nations to bring about change and stand up for the voices of women.

Pīwakawaka, Kate Sheppard, and Meri Mangakahia bear witness to my days and remind me that I am stronger than I think. They remind me to lift up and support other women and to be a voice allied with the silenced and marginalized.

The editors of Minerva Rising have brought together the voices of women writers in this issue to mark the centennial of the 19th Amendment to the USA Constitution. While we celebrate the women that have gone on before us, it is also essential to remember the reality that women are still fighting 100 years later for equality. While we want to honor the centennial, we recognize that it has a complicated legacy of who benefited and those whom it left out. Even after the historic election of Vice President Harris, it is still important to face the fact that women, especially Black, Indigenous, and women of color, are denied leadership positions in companies, lack body autonomy and reproductive rights, and are paid less than their male colleagues.

We may celebrate women's right to vote, but voter suppression persists despite the Voting Rights Act of 1965, primarily targeting LGBTQ, immigrants, disabled, and BIPOC (Black, Indigenous, and people of color) voters. Our fight for equality isn't over, I'd like to say it is just beginning, but it has been 100 years. This collection is to honor the journey of 100 years that brought us here and the path we need to forge ahead. We will not be silenced.

With deep gratitude, I thank the authors of the pieces selected for this issue of Minerva Rising. You are continuing the story of the important women in our world, whether they are famous suffragettes or the legendary women who raised us, taught us, mentored us. We hold the narratives of generations in our bodies; we sing the stories of our ancestors; we keep the pain that life brings; we harvest the wisdom from the collective of women that support and build us up.

We have a voice. And it is time to listen to it.

Rebecca Beardsall
Creative Nonfiction Editor

Dream Logic

Rosalind Kaplan

In the moments when you were dying, I was 80 miles away, examining a young woman's swollen ankle in a sterile, blue-white exam room under glaring fluorescents lights. Her ankle was improving, reassuring me that the antibiotics I'd prescribed days earlier were working. She was my only patient that morning, the morning of Christmas Eve, 1990.

In my mind, I see your bedroom, the room in which you died that morning. There are shafts of gray light auguring light snow, peeking through the slats of the vertical blinds on the windows flanking the dark wood headboard. The walls and carpet are a tasteful, unobtrusive ecru. The headboard is against the far wall, the matching bureau to the right of the door.

I see you waking in your place on the left side of the bed, your side, with its two pillows covered in lilac-colored pillowcases. I see the crumpled lilac sheets and patterned pastel comforter over your lower body as you sit up in your white cotton nightgown, your short dark curls wild around your face. But the image stops there.

I can't see your expression. I can't hear the words Dad told me you spoke: "Call 911, I'm dying." I can't envision the gestures you might have made. Did you hold your chest, fist to sternum, in the 'universal sign for chest pain'? Did you clutch your head or neck? Did your eyes go wide with fear or surprise?

I can't see you slump back on the lilac pillows, pulseless and pallid, though I imagine this is what happened.

I imagine this part only in words. I find the words and write them down, but the images don't appear in my mind's eye.

Did Dad believe your words? Did he pick up the phone while you still had blood pulsing through your arteries? He wouldn't have tried to breathe life back into you or press on your chest, trying to keep your heart in motion, because he didn't know how to perform CPR.

Weeks later, when I asked for details, he told me, "I don't remember."

I try to see, to hear, to know, but I will never know. I wasn't there. I was in a cold, glaring blue-white room, examining a young woman's swollen ankle. She was fine, but you weren't.

You were leaving the world, leaving me.

My mother's sudden death has been one of the 'defining moments' in my life. She was 62 years old and was not sick, had no medical problems except high blood pressure, for which she took medication. I was 30, a new doctor, a new mother. I remember the phone call with my father in a distorted, slowed-down, time-release way. "Your mother has had a massive heart attack." Right after the words 'heart attack,' I knew she was dead, and I handed the phone to my husband, Larry, who stood next to me when I took the call.

I'd headed home after seeing only one patient in the medical office where Larry and I worked because it was the beginning of a holiday. Only urgent visits had been scheduled. Anita, the secretary Larry and I shared, who referred to us as Mrs. Dr. Kaplan and Mr. Dr. Kaplan, had tracked me down after my father called the office. Anita said, "Your father told me it wasn't an emergency. But if he called here on a holiday, I thought it must be important." So she called me at home.

After I found out my mother was dead, I said to my Dad, "Why did you tell Anita it wasn't an emergency?" Then I realized it wasn't. She was already dead.

I think of defining moments as the ones that I remember, no matter how long ago they occurred, as though they happened yesterday, or this morning, or five minutes ago. They are the moments that took my breath, bowling balls hitting my solar plexus. Moments for which I have crystal clear recall of my surroundings and activities years after the fact: JFK's assassination, 9/11, my mother's death.

I was only three years old when JFK was shot, yet I remember the events, or think I do, as they occurred in my child's world. I was playing in my bedroom, sitting on the floor near my iron trundle bed. Across the hall, my mother folded laundry while she watched our black-and-white RCA TV set with the rabbit ear antennae. I heard a sudden gasp, and then my mother crying. Sobbing. That's how I remember it.

I was afraid to move, afraid to go into her room. But after some unclear amount of time, she came to me and explained that the president had died. I still didn't understand why she was crying. We didn't know the president.

On the morning of September 11, 2001, I was in another exam room, decorated in the dark wood and mauve textiles favored by designers of doctors' offices at the time, a palette intended to appear non-threatening, to calm anxious patients. I was in the midst of performing a physical exam when my nurse knocked and summoned me out of the room. She told me that planes had hit the Twin Towers in Manhattan, that possibly something had also happened in Washington, DC. She'd heard this on the radio. Nobody knew what it all meant yet.

The phone in my office started ringing wildly in the next few minutes. My children's schools, telling me they were safe. I could pick them up early if I chose to. My husband, asking if I knew, if I was okay. A friend who could not reach her sister in Manhattan.

The radio chattered on with new but unconfirmed information. It felt as though the world was experiencing a sandstorm. Everyone was blinded in this storm. We waited for the wind to stop so we could assess the damage, but the gusts blew for days.

The gusts from my mother's death lasted years for me. My mother knew my first child, Max, for only three months. He'd entered the world that September. His birth was chaotic, by emergency caesarian section, a sudden turn in the middle of a difficult labor. Doctors and nurses yelled commands, pulled him out of me in a sterile surgical field. I was numb from the waist down. After an initial surge of fear, I was also emotionally numb.

Max spent a week in the neonatal intensive care unit, after turning blue in the nursery the night of his birth, a week during which I remained insensate until we were finally released from the hospital.

At home, Max was an unusually alert, almost vigilant baby. He suffered from what we called 'colic' then, screaming for hours from the late afternoon into the evening for the first few months of his life. Now my pediatrician friends say that he probably had acid reflux; they give babies antacid for this and say it works wonders. Back then, all we could do was walk the floors with him and wait for time to pass.

I was a weepy, frightened, shell-shocked mother in those first months, though I could look competent when necessary. I was too insecure to nurse Max in front of people. I didn't sleep at night, afraid he would stop breathing again. I didn't know what to do with an infant who stared at me, wide-eyed, as though waiting for something to happen, whenever he was awake. I carried him in a Snugli and read the *New York Times* aloud to him in a high-pitched, hysterical tone. I often wanted to give him back, but there was no return policy.

My mother, though, was in love with Max from the minute she first saw him. She told me from the beginning that he was extraordinary.

"I'm not just saying that because he's my grandson. He's special. He's brilliant." My mother was a child psychologist. I wanted to believe that she actually knew something that no one else did, but I had no evidence. As adorable as my blue-eyed baby was, I worried that the colic and his hypoxic episode in the hospital foretold some defect, some impending disaster.

At the time my mother died, the colic was just starting to dissipate. I was back at work as a doctor and assistant professor at one of the Philadelphia area medical schools, regaining my footing in the world. I was developing some confidence in my parenting. I finally felt bonded with my baby. I believed my world was safe again.

My mother's death sent me hurtling back into the stratosphere. If she could suddenly drop dead, then anything and everything catastrophic was possible at any moment.

During the time I spent with my father in New Jersey, I learned that he was not at all certain that my mother had died from a heart attack. He only knew that she had told him she was dying. It could have been her heart, or it could have been a stroke or a ruptured aneurysm. My father chose not to get an autopsy. I'll never know what really happened. I suppose it doesn't matter, except to quiet my mind.

Sometimes I have macabre fantasies: that she died by suicide, and my father was covering it up. I have even wondered if my father killed her. But I don't believe my own imaginings: my father was an extremely gentle and honest person. I don't believe he was a murderer. I don't believe it was his fault. It's just difficult to accept an explanation that explains nothing.

After my mother's funeral and the ritual week of Jewish mourning, I came back to my home in Philadelphia. I returned to my routine of seeing patients, teaching, caring for my baby, making dinners, being with my husband. I pushed through. I pretended that nothing had changed. But my world felt unsafe. Soon I lived in a 'new normal' life, a shaky equilibrium, something that looked like recovery, though it was really just a holding pattern.

The first dream I had about you made me wonder if I was crazy, or some kind of misguided psychic. The dream came in October, when Max was just a little more than a year old. You visited me from the world of the dead. I couldn't see you, but I could hear you. I knew you were there, a disembodied spirit. You returned because you wanted Max with you in the world of the dead. Somehow, that wasn't unreasonable in the dream, but it wasn't acceptable to me, and I argued with you. I said you couldn't have him, and you told me I didn't have a choice. This was as far as our negotiation went.

I woke with a start out of that dream to the insistent ringing of the phone.

It was 6:30 am, and my husband's father was on the other end. Just an hour earlier, Larry's sister had found her 2-month-old son, Andrew, cold and blue in his crib. Later it was determined that he'd died from Sudden Infant Death Syndrome.

I told no one about my dream. I secretly felt that Andrew's death was my fault. My mother had wanted Max and I wouldn't give him up to her. Awake, I imagined I'd somehow won the argument with my mother in the dream, and she'd taken our nephew instead. There was no logic to these thoughts. My dream logic was so powerful that it drove my waking thoughts.

The weekend before my mother died, she asked me for something, and I refused her.

Larry and Max and I were visiting with Larry's parents in Central New Jersey, and my parents had joined us all at their home on Sunday afternoon. When it was time for my parents to leave, Max was napping in his Pack 'n Play crib.

"Could I wake him, just for a moment, to say goodbye?" my mother asked me.

"Mom, no! Nobody wakes a sleeping baby." I replied.

"Just for a minute. He'll go back to sleep."

"No. He'll be up if you wake him." The truth was, I needed the break. I was thinking of myself.

Instead, she snuck into the room where he slept, and watched him sleep for a minute. Then she left. It was the last time I saw my mother alive, and the last time my mother saw my son.

She wanted to say goodbye. 'Goodbye' is a strong word. Why not 'goodnight'? Did she know something? *Did you, Mom? Did you know something then? Should I have known something?*

In my first days at home after Max's birth, my mother tried to help me adjust, to relax into motherhood, to get over my fears. She came to Philly and stayed for a few days when he was just a couple of weeks old. She held him while I showered. She helped with laundry and cooking while I nursed him. She helped me find a nanny to give me respite for a few hours a day until I went back to work, and then to care for Max while I was at work. Then she left abruptly, telling me I needed to 'get back to my life.' I was still a mess. I wasn't ready for her to leave.

"You need to go back to work," she told me. "You'll feel better, more normal, when you do. Don't get caught in the kiddie coop like I did."

Don't get caught in the kiddie coop? That wasn't going to happen- I was going back to work three days a week after six weeks of maternity leave. I worked hard for my MD and gave up three years of sleep and leisure to do my medical residency. That was not all going to waste.

I agreed with her that I needed to go back to work. Nevertheless, I took her comment as a rejection. Had she not loved me and my brother when we were babies? Did she resent caring for us when we were little?

My mother had started graduate school years earlier, right out of college, but against her parents' wishes. She worked delivering telephone books to pay her tuition and chose a degree in education as teaching was an acceptable vocation for women in the 1950's. It wasn't the career she wanted, and soon the push to get married and settled down, before she became an 'old maid,' caught up to her. Her marriage to my father in 1958 ended her time as a working woman.

When I was three years old, she returned to school for a doctorate in psychology. She spent two afternoons a week taking classes at Rutgers University, half an hour from our home, and wrote her entire doctoral thesis longhand on our varnished fruitwood dining room table in her 'spare time,' while simultaneously caring for me and my brother. My father, who worked long hours and traveled frequently as an editor at a prominent scientific publishing company, rarely was around to help our with childcare.

Ten years later, some of her work could still be seen etched into the shiny wood of that table. When the table was replaced by the Danish teak furniture popular in the 70's, I felt a nostalgia for the old, well-used piece. But I didn't realize then that the etching in the tabletop was evidence of the compromises my mother made to have both her children and her chosen career. It is only now that I can grasp how much she wanted both.

The morning of that first dream about my mother, I didn't have a lot of time to think about it as we quickly left for Connecticut to attend our nephew's funeral. After his death, our extended family was declared a 'SIDS family.' Larry had a brother who had died of SIDS 30 years earlier. The doctors thought that Max's hypoxic episode may have some relationship to this. Andrew's death had not, of course, been my fault.

Still, the timing of the dream was uncanny. I wished I had an explanation. Back then I still believed that the world, and my own experiences, should make sense.

The second dream is recurrent. You have returned to the living world. I don't know how I know this, but I know you are back, as though back from a long trip abroad, before cell phones and emails made communication across the world possible. You look the same in this dream as you always did to me-sturdy, your hair a mass of dark curls that, even after 60, even after death, only have a few random silver strands, but your face deeply lined with stress and worry. I know you look like this, but in the dream, I am not with you. I long to see you. I have so much to say, so much to tell you, so much to ask. I want to know what happened, where you have been, why you left.

It is all I want, all I have seemed to want forever, in this dream, but you refuse me. I try to call, frantically try to reach you, and you don't answer. You are out there, but I can't find you, and you have somehow let me know that you will see my brother, you will be with other people, but you don't want to see me. You want nothing to do with me.

I have had this dream many times. Sleep experts and psychiatrists and scientists now write that dreams in themselves mean nothing. They're just a way for the brain to dump excess information from our waking hours. The images in the dreams are, in essence, detritus, and if we choose to interpret them, we are simply making things up.

If that is true, why do we dream recurrently? Why is the dream of arriving for a test, having forgotten to study, or unable to find the right room a dream that is common to people who have gone to school? Why are dreams of being chased, or of falling, seemingly ubiquitous?

I can't dismiss the dream about my mother. She rejects me, abandons me again and again and again in my dreamscape. I awake from it exhausted, grieving, anguished. It takes hours for my psyche to adjust to the idea that it didn't actually happen. I know it has to mean something.

After years of working part-time in mental-health clinics while my brother and I attended school, my mother finally amassed enough hours of supervision as a psychotherapist to become licensed. When I was in Middle School, she began her own psychology practice in an office off the main hallway of our home.

I would sometimes sneak in and read her textbooks when she wasn't there. I wanted to know what she knew, what she did in her office with those other people, many of them children, while her own children were just a few steps away in the kitchen or den. I don't know if my mother knew that I was reading her textbooks. I'm not even sure why I kept it a secret; perhaps I thought she would forbid it, saying the information was inappropriate for someone my age. Looking back now, though, I doubt it. More likely, I felt like I shouldn't be treading on my mother's sacred professional ground. She didn't talk about her work with her clients, and I might have believed that it was the whole of psychology, not just the client information, that was a deep, dark secret.

In some ways, psychology was a deep, dark secret in our family. I would not find out until much later that both my parents suffered with depression in adulthood. I knew that my brother struggled socially, and was sometimes hard to get along with, but he was also very smart, so his Attention Deficit Hyperactivity Disorder was not diagnosed until we were adults. These issues always lurked under the surface of my 'normal', two-parent, suburban, upper-middle class life, like a shark circling, waiting to surface and attack. Still, I knew nothing consciously until I was an adult.

My own depression and anxiety didn't officially present until I was an adult, but I know now that, as a child, I was unusually anxious. Nobody ever told me that it wasn't 'normal' to worry constantly, to be afraid to be away from my family overnight, to need the light on in the hallway, the door to my room open in order to fall asleep, to obsess about being 'bad' when, in fourth grade, I accidentally damaged a school textbook by getting crayon marks in it.

That my own mother was doing psychotherapy with other children and adults but didn't question her own daughter's discomfort living in the world, is a sad irony, one that, I think, speaks to my mother's distraction as she tried to navigate through her busy and complicated world.

As a young child, I craved time and attention from my mother. I didn't pursue it the way some children did, by being a squeaky wheel. Instead, I tried to be good, to not make trouble, and hoped I would be rewarded by having my needs noticed.

My mother would come into my room to kiss me goodnight, and I always wanted her to stay, sitting on my bed, talking to me, for longer than she did, but she always seemed to have something more important to do.

In elementary school, we went home from school for lunch and returned afterward. I was a latch-key child. I wished that she would be home at lunchtime like the other mothers, instead of leaving my lunch for me in the refrigerator, to be eaten in front of the television and that she, instead of an after-school babysitter, would be there after school.

Soon I gave up and retreated to television, books, and playing outside in our cul-de-sac with the neighborhood kids. I begged for a dog, which I never got, but pretended that my gerbils and guppies were 'real pets.' I practiced my flute, hoping to be as good a musician as my brother, but I didn't have the talent.

Finally, in high school, I settled for being a straight-A student, a reasonably good ballet and jazz dancer, and a social butterfly. It didn't make my mother pay more attention to me, but by high school, having a less attentive mother had its perks.

Maybe it was my childhood wish for more attention that triggered my recurrent dream of her rejection. Or maybe it was my fantasy that, if she knew what my life was like without her, she would be angry.

When she died, my father gave me her silk scarves and her pearls and the diamond from her engagement ring. I took the beautiful things that had belonged to her. They were given to me; I didn't earn them. I had taken her time and her energy and as much of her attention as I could get. And I got so much in life that she'd wanted but couldn't quite have.

I didn't have to struggle and compromise to get my education. When I chose medicine, my parents not only gave me their blessing but also paid my entire medical school tuition.

I had children and also got recognition for my work. I had a husband who shared the load at home, who didn't leave me to diaper the babies while he moved up the corporate ladder.

And I found time to write, to publish a book, to attend writing conferences, all of which my mother, a natural writer herself would have loved.

And finally, maybe most importantly, I haven't had a difficult mother to struggle with my entire adult life.

My maternal grandmother, Helen, was a force to be reckoned with. My mother's stories of her childhood were tales of emotional deprivation and cruelty: her mother telling her she was not pretty enough to have more than two dresses to wear to school, checking her ears and fingernails for dirt in front of her friends, giving away my mother's dog while she was at school one day because it had urinated in the house. She didn't tell me any of this until I was an adult. She needed me to love my grandmother so that my grandmother could love me.

My own experience of Helen when I was a child was ambivalent. My grandparents spoiled me in the typical way, buying me toys and clothes and letting me have ice cream every night during a visit to their home in Ohio, but I somehow knew that it was all predicated on my being 'good.' I was a quiet and orderly child most of the time, but if I stepped out of line, roughhousing with my brother or having a tantrum when I was over-tired, the disapproval was palpable. The air would immediately take on a chill. I was always a little afraid when I was with my grandmother.

Throughout my childhood and adolescence, my mother talked to her parents on the phone at least once a week, except when there was a falling out. Periodically, maybe once or twice a year, my mother and grandmother would have an explosive fight, either at the end of a visit or over the phone. Then they would stop speaking, and my mother would cry every day. I either never knew, or have conveniently forgotten, what those fights were about.

Eventually, my mother would become exhausted and give in, though she never felt she should. My grandmother's will was as strong as a diamond and as sharp as a razor blade. Resolution and the return to normalcy required repeated apologies from my mother, flowers sent

to Ohio, acquiescence to whatever terms Helen dictated. While I wasn't there to witness it, my father told me that the pattern continued after I left home, and that my mother was arguing with her parents only a couple of days before she died.

As a teenager, I wondered why my mother was always the one to fold. Why didn't she just tell Helen to take a hike? My mother was a professional woman with a home and a family and money of her own. Why would she let someone hurt her like that, make her cry, and then make her beg and plead for forgiveness for something she hadn't done?

If I have learned nothing else from losing my mother at a young age, I have learned this: she let it happen because she needed her mother.

Had my mother lived longer, I don't think we would have had the tumultuous, toxic, and painful relationship with each other that she and Helen had. Not that our relationship was easy; Because I felt she'd often been emotionally absent when I was young, I sometimes blamed that, blamed her, for the anxiety and depression I battled off and on as a young adult. I also felt she resented me at times. She confirmed this for me by saying, when we did clash, that I was 'selfish' and 'entitled.' In my teens and early 20's I knew definitively that those were two of the worst traits a person- no, a *woman*- could have. But in the last couple of years before her death, we started to let go of the ways in which we had disappointed each other. I think we stopped looking for the hurt and started finding some grace.

What would my life be like if you were still here? Would I have fought and struggled with you? Would I have felt smothered by you or beholden to you? Would I resent caring for you in old age, as many of my friends now resent their parents at the end of their long lives?

Maybe so. But I also would have had your company, your support when you had it to give, the wisdom you had and imparted in tiny aliquots through my life. Remember when I was ten, and I worried a lot? You told me to set aside a half an hour a day for worrying, and then worry hard during that time, but not any other time. I don't think I ever told you that it actually worked.

If you had stuck around, my children would have had you as a grandmother who loved them with sheer abandonment, the way you loved Max for those few months. That would have been good for them.

I did okay with my kids, but I could have used your help. I didn't know what I was doing, and I had to make it all up as I went along. Max is brilliant, by the way. It's hard raising a kid who's too smart for his own good. Maddy is unusually sensitive. Maybe like you. Like me. That was hard, too. I hope I gave them what they needed to thrive.

I could have used a parent when I was depressed, when I was sick, when I was unsure. I know you couldn't give me as much as I wanted, but I would have taken whatever you were able to give.

You left me too soon. I still needed you. I ended up okay, but I still needed you.

My daughter, Maddy, now 25, brought me a gift the last time she visited: a delicate silver chain with a rose gold charm. The charm is in the shape of a hat with cat ears, a representation of the 'pink pussy hat' that many of the participants in the 2017 Women's March on Washington, DC wore. I was in DC that day, wearing my hand-knitted bright pink hat, the ears a bit asymmetrical, demonstrating my less-than-optimal knitting skills. Maddy knew how proud I was to be part of that march, so when she saw this necklace in a shop, she decided to buy it for me, especially when she found out that part of the proceeds from its sale benefited a charity that assists victims of sexual violence.

When I opened the box it came in, a memory from more than 20 years ago drifted over me.

March 1986. I was in medical school in Philadelphia. The March for Women's Lives, a rally for reproductive rights to be held in Washington, DC, was coming up, and was expected to be massive. I planned to go and mentioned this to my mother. She was 58 at the time, the same age I am now. She asked, "May I go with you?"

I was surprised, as she never liked big crowds. I fretted a bit about how she'd cope, especially if the weather turned bad. I warned her about the long bus ride we would have to take, the paucity of clean bathrooms, the need to bring

our own food and water, the long day and sore feet we would likely have, but she still wanted to go.

I needn't have worried. My mother was right in her element, holding up a sign saying 'Mothers for Choice,' chanting, marching, sitting on the grass on the Mall, and cheering during speeches given by NOW leadership.

How could I have forgotten? This was who my mother was. She was someone who cared about issues, about women, about equality and fairness. Someone who had given part of her life to improving the lives of others through her work, someone who had done the best she could to raise two children to be moral people, someone who put together the best life she could for herself despite the obstacles her family and the times and society put in front of her.

I had another dream about you that night after Maddy gave me the necklace. You look like you did before you died, not old or frail, but I know, in the dream, that you are older. I am in your house in New Jersey with you. In the dream, I am myself, the age I am now. The house has too much furniture in it. So much furniture in some of the rooms that it is hard to walk around it. The furniture includes what you had in your house, but also some of the furniture from my house, and some from your mother's house.

I tell you that I want to move the furniture around so that it fits better, and that maybe we don't need all of it. I think you are going to protest, to tell me it is your house and you don't want me changing it. But you don't. You say, "Go ahead. You can do what you think is best." You sit there, watching, while I rearrange things. When I'm done, you agree that the new way is better.

Perhaps dreams don't really mean anything in themselves. Maybe some of us just interpret this 'junk,' this mental detritus, to make meaning out of the detritus of our lives. For me, it doesn't matter; over time, my dreams have helped me make peace with losing my mother in such a strange, seemingly meaningless way, a way that afforded no opportunity for any resolution between us. They have allowed me to see my mother in all her complexity, to appreciate what was good, and forgive the rest.

Thirteen Ways of Mothering

Emily Bowles

I am so Prudent, and Careful of my Poor Labours, which are my Writing Works, as I always keep the Copies of them safely with me, until they are Printed, and then I Commit the Originals to the Fire, like Parents which are willing to Die, whenas they are sure of their Childrens Lives, knowing when they are Old, and past Breeding, they are but Useless in this World.

— Margaret Cavendish

This baby-body of mine rebirthed me, mother in a way,
her fingernails fragment that fell me fondly, mothering away.

Every bildungsroman becomes a story of unbecoming when she
marries [Jo March, Anne Shirley, Meg Murry], mother throw away.

I was married once or twice or maybe three times, hurtingly, heavily:
Aunt Jennifer with her tigers, I threw the mother ring away.

White is not just___for weddings; Emily dressed it, pressed it with wild
night wordings, shipless moorings, feathering *Gentlest mother*ing her way.

Every woman read to me, reading me, gives birth differently:
Cavendish's paper bodies, each writer my mother in her way.

Gilman's rest cure, milk in bed, wallpaper moving, babies are
revolting—think it, and doctor orders disorder, smothering away.

My worth measured worst measure wasted, waist thickening
until I am not recognizable as myself/a self, mothering I weigh.

Every posture is performance, each mirror unmasking what is
not, naked fingers (mine) on a mat, other mother rings pray.

We women run together, in groups that expand beyond the sidewalk, safety
that breeds a different danger, lanes of bodies, mothers in the way.

PTA meetings forgotten, dinners burnt, laundry left unfolded,
and a tear I should have seen, unhappily mothering my way.

Every pot on my porch is full of dying, dirt diminishing, while she put loving hands on bleeding hearts, Walker's mother gardening away.

Name it—the value we place on it—labor that goes unpaid, "the shitwork of humanity," "I want a wife"—we look at mothering another way.

We are living smaller, stuck together, domestic disorder reigns,
refrains that mean we refrain and inside, we are mothering away. ●

Margaret the First

Though I cannot be Henry the Fifth, or Charles the Second; yet, I will endeavour to be, Margaret the First.

— Margaret Cavendish (1688)

1.

She was not my first
Margaret.

2.

Woolf made her into a character—object, abject—asking "what could bind, tame, or civilize
for human use
that wild, generous, untutored intelligence" that "poured itself out, higgledy-piggledy."
Books like hers, of hers have sense been bound for human use, taught and studied, and that
"wild, generous, untutored intelligence" has been written, rewritten as indicative of a
literary, philosophical, scientific brain. Still, she is only a character, our character bound
by our needs, what we're looking for in a literary foremother (she had not children; paper
bodies she called her books her babies, and there's a sadness in it and also a recognition that
the sadness may be our own extrapolation—her husband bred horses and was very old).

3.
She was not my first
Margaret,
but that Other Woman named Margaret helped me eventually find her: a professor named
Margaret, she was "as Ambitious as ever any of [her] Sex was," the most prolifically published
scholar at a time when women were expected to wear glass slippers not rule in ivory towers.

4.
And then I had so many more

Margarets:
Atwood Drabble Fuller Mead Mitchell Sanger Rozga

5.
I am a mother now, with fewer paper bodies surrounding me, and Margaret Wise Brown
books in my closet, a voice of a story that was my daughter years ago, a story I read to her,
told her again and again, and when I look at those pages again, I am Woolf wanting to bind
her up, refusing to believe what another Margaret knew/knows: "If it's a story I'm telling, then

I have control over the ending," says Offred/said Atwood, "Then there will be an ending, to the story, and real life will come after it." No stories have endings. Bound, unbound, each Margaret exists alone and apart,

a part of my story, words I wish were my own, which are "higgledy-piggledy" echoes and imitations

of Margaret_____

my first. ◉

What My Mom Told Me

Lisa Zimmerman

After a photo collage by Kayo Peeler

If clothes make the man, do shoes make the woman?
My grandma was a suffragette, wore flat heeled lace-up boots
made by her cousin, hand-tooled with hidden steel toes.
Mom told me Grandma kicked a man who tried to wrench
the VOTES FOR WOMEN sign from her hands
as she marched with her sisters, and he didn't try again.
Mom says her high heels hurt her feet but she wears them
with tailored wool suits to her job downtown, typing
75 words a minute in the insurance office on 10th Street.
She's proud her wages helped to buy our house, the new
Dixie stove, my red leather shoes that stay snug
when I race across the gravel schoolyard,
faster than all the boys, even the older ones.
I always let out a big whoop, nothing ahead of me
but a short metal fence under the big blue sky,
because Mom says it's okay to be fast,
to be first, to be heard.

OUR BODIES OUR STREETS

Ehimetalor Akhere Unuabona

Women of To-Day

Violet Snow

From the historical novel To March or to Marry

Washington, DC, 1917

Their leader, Alice Paul, could have designed Broadway shows, thought Louise, who was bringing up the end of the line. She watched the row of purple, white, and gold banners making their way down Madison Place after leaving the National Woman's Party headquarters. The dark branches of the sidewalk trees released golden leaves that floated down, tasteful accents matching the gold of the banners. The somber women looked straight ahead as they marched the short block past Lafayette Park to the White House. The banners, like tricolor sails of a ship, billowed bright against the ironwork of the fencing as the women spread out on either side of the gate, two lettered banners hoisted among them. Jessie had asked for the honor of holding the one that read, "HOW LONG MUST WOMEN WAIT FOR LIBERTY?", reported to be the final words of Inez Milholland, who had died on a speaking tour the year before and was now celebrated as a martyr to the suffrage cause.

There were three four-hour shifts each day, from eight in the morning to eight at night. The women never knew when the police would decide to swoop down on them, but Louise had learned to gauge the mood of the crowd and the police. If she sensed either group growing agitated, she suggested taking the next day off, and twice in October she and Jessie missed getting arrested. Jessie had been appalled by the poverty of women she served while working at the Henry Street Settlement in New York. She agreed with people who felt women voters were required if the country was to change the laws that oppressed the poor. If it took incarceration of protestors to convince the American public that women should have the vote, Jessie was willing and eager to throw her lot in with those getting arrested. Louise, however, thought it wise to give Jessie time to adjust to the rigors of suffrage life before heading off to jail. Louise was only four years older than her friend,

but Jessie's sheltered life had offered considerably less hardship than her own.

At twenty-four, Jessie was blossoming, invigorated by the novelty of visiting Washington, of picketing, of camaraderie with bold women. Upon returning from the silent picket line, they sat at the Cameron House headquarters, drinking tea in a group of women who chatted, joked, cursed, and read news articles aloud, with discussion following. Each evening, Louise and Jessie retreated to the little room they shared at a boarding-house catering to suffs. They weren't getting paid, but they both had money saved up from working, and Louise made sure Jessie ate well.

Miss Paul had been in the hospital for a month that summer with a suspected case of Bright's disease, an often fatal kidney ailment. Having been misdiagnosed, she emerged intact, though weak. Her lieutenants kept her off the picket line for a few weeks, insisting she recover her strength. She appeared in September, bearing a banner that compared President Wilson to Kaiser Wilhelm for claiming to fight for freedom while refusing to give women the freedom to vote. She was knocked down three times and a sailor dragged her across the street, trying to tear off her tricolor sash. The police seized 148 of the silk and linen banners, and six women were arrested. To the suffs' relief, Miss Paul was not among them. On October 6, however, she was finally arrested and received a suspended sentence. It seemed to Louise they were all holding their breath, knowing their leader would make her way into prison at some point.

On October 20, Louise and Jessie went out on the morning shift. They wore rubber coats against a fine drizzle that set the banners off with a soft gray aura. The pickets lined up in front of the White House with a banner that quoted the president's speech about entering the war: "THE TIME HAS COME TO CONQUER OR SUBMIT. FOR US THERE CAN BE BUT ONE

CHOICE—WE HAVE MADE IT." One passerby called out, "Keep at it, girls!" Another, an old man with a crutch, told them, "You'll make it, I'm sure." Then a sailor spit on the banner, prompting Jessie to shout, strictly against the rules, "You know, those are the president's words you're spitting on." He stopped and gave her a push that made her stagger back, while a policeman pointedly looked the other way. The sailor spit on her shoes and walked off. Louise, worried, examined Jessie's face and saw her swallow her shock and anger, compose herself, and step back into the line.

The gates opened, and a long black automobile slid through from the street, carrying President Wilson back from his daily round of golf. Some days, he tipped his hat at the pickets, while his wife sat beside him, glaring at them. Today, both of the Wilsons looked straight ahead as they rode past. The gates closed behind the automobile.

At noon, the next shift of women came marching down Madison at their usual slow, solemn pace. "That's Miss Paul at the front," murmured Jessie. The woman's thin, pale face wore the look of a warrior.

"You're right," said Louise. She had an intuition it was Miss Paul's day to be arrested.

"Should we stay?" Jessie asked.

"No, I don't think so. We're scheduled to go back."

They handed over their banners to the newcomers and returned to headquarters. An hour later, they were in the midst of tea and sandwiches, when a woman ran in, shouting, "They've arrested Miss Paul and Miss Spencer!"

"Oh, no!" Jessie said.

"It's what she wants," Louise reassured her. "It'll make the papers for sure, with a big headline just because it's Miss Paul."

"I feel bad, though. She's in there, and we're out here. Oh, why can't we get arrested?"

Alice Paul was given seven months in the District jail, the longest sentence yet. "The judge is making an example of her," said Dora Lewis, who took charge in Miss Paul's absence. "She's going to insist on being treated as a political prisoner, which would mean visitation rights and keeping her own clothes and being allowed to read and write."

"Do you think it will be granted?" asked Jessie.

"No. She may go on hunger strike in protest."

"But she was in the hospital not so long ago. She might die."

"Wilson can't afford to let her die. The publicity would destroy him. They'll either let her out or forcibly feed her."

"I don't see how they could stick a tube down the nose of that gentle little woman."

Mrs. Lewis snorted. "Oh, yes, gentle like a tiger."

At Cameron House, anyone planning to picket was given a thorough warning on the experience of past pickets and what might happen to those arrested in the future. Miss Paul wanted only committed women on the line, who were strong enough to deal with the consequences and couldn't complain they didn't know what was coming.

Hunger strike was presented as an option for those arrested. Pinned to the office wall was a copy of an article from *New York World Magazine* by journalist Djuna Barnes, who had voluntarily submitted to force-feeding, just to see what it was like. Jessie read the article over and over, once reading passages aloud to Louise.

Unbidden visions of remote horrors danced madly through my mind. There arose the hideous thought of being gripped in the tentacles of some monster devil fish in the depths of a tropic sea, as the liquid slowly sensed its way along innumerable endless passages....

I had lapsed into a physical mechanism without power to oppose or resent the outrage to my will.

Jessie was awed by the audacity of a woman who had done nothing to merit punishment and yet subjected herself to excruciating pain just to report on the experience other women had gone through. Louise didn't know what to make of Jessie's interest. Was it a fantasy of personal heroism or a morbid focus on suffering? At some point, Jessie would surely be tested. Louise just hoped to be at her side to shepherd her through.

Suffs released from the District jail reported that Miss Paul had thrown, and incited other prisoners to throw, objects—tin cups, light bulbs, even her accurately tossed volume of Browning's poetry—in an effort to break the closed windows high up on the walls of the airless cells. As a result, she had been placed in solitary confinement. Then Miss Paul and Rose Winslow, the scrappy Polish-American labor organizer, ended up in the hospital wing because they were so weak from lack of exercise and from eating the wormy pork and greasy broth that passed for food.

On November 6, the woman suffrage referendum passed in New York, the first eastern state to add its women to the ranks of female voters. The milestone had come despite predictions that the picketing would turn the state's voters against suffrage. The rejoicing at Cameron House was muted by the knowledge that Miss Paul was waning in strength.

Meanwhile, women from eleven states traveled to Washington to protest her incarceration. Dora Lewis called a meeting at Cameron House. "Before Miss Paul was arrested," she explained, "she told me we'd have to stop the picketing soon because it was becoming stale news. Her idea was to have one final demonstration with a mass of people that would clog the justice system. With the visitors from the states, we have a sufficient number. How many women here are prepared to picket tomorrow and get arrested?"

"It's our last chance," Jessie whispered to Louise. "This time, we have to stay out until the police grab us, no matter what."

"Yes, you're right. We'll do it."

Their hands went up, along with thirty-nine others.

Someone suggested going to the jail and standing under Miss Paul's window. A cleaning woman had been smuggling information out, so they knew where her room was and that she had started a hunger strike. In a dank courtyard, permeated with smells of mold and soot, the women stood on rubble-strewn dirt. Each one shouted up her name and the state she had come from. Mrs. Lewis called out the information that the National Women's Party had received a flood of donations, and the forty-one women now in the courtyard would be protesting tomorrow.

"I'm being forcibly fed three times a day," Miss Paul called down. "It's worse than in England. There it was only twice a day."

"She's so noble," Jessie sighed. "I could never be like her."

"No one could," Louise replied.

"Hey, you!" came a shout, and a squad of guards hustled the women back out to the street.

The government workers were going home for lunch, women and men in their fall coats pouring along the sidewalk outside the White House gates, many of them saluting the pickets as they went by. Two patrol wagons pulled up. The policemen seized the banners and herded the fifteen women into the vans, while the spectators applauded, as they often did during arrests. Louise wasn't sure how many were clapping for the police and how many for the suffs, but today the mood seemed sympathetic to the pickets. Jessie was the last to climb into the wagon, and as she was sitting down on the bench, they heard the spectators saying, "Look! More of them!"

"The second group is coming," Jessie said, peeking out the door. "Mrs. Lewis was sending ten, I think." Soon five more women were added to their wagon, and the back door closed. Another wagon would have to be sent for the other five. The police had no idea three more groups were waiting to head out to the White House.

The women spent the night on mats on the floor of the District House of Detention. The next day in court, several who had been arrested repeatedly were given sentences of anywhere from sixty days to six months. Louise and Jessie each got fifteen days. Off they went to Occoquan Workhouse and what came to be known as the Night of Terror.

We refuse to give our names to anyone but the workhouse superintendent," said Dora Lewis, appointed by the prisoners to speak for them. She was a widow in her fifties, bold, articulate, and a natural leader.

"Superintendent Whittaker is out," Minnie Herndon, the matron, said, her consonants crisp and forceful. "You'll have to sit here all night. He may not be back for two or three days."

"We will await his return," Mrs. Lewis replied.

The room was stuffy and brightly lit. The women sat in chairs lined up in rows, facing the matron's desk. She read out their names in a roll call, but no one responded.

"You'd better answer up, or it'll be the worse for you," said a male guard – one of five lounging against the wall.

The man next to him strolled to the back of the room, where Lucy Burns, a redheaded fireball, sat with her eyes closed. "I'll handle you, so you'll be sorry," the man said, leaning over her. She did not open her eyes.

The women had been told to expect threats of violence from the prison staff, but past experience had showed they were generally bluffing. Louise tried to keep calm, inspired by Miss Burns and Mrs. Lewis, knowing she had to be a model for Jessie, who was trembling next to her. She wanted to hold Jessie's hand but didn't want to attract the guards' attention. A cluster of men stood in the hallway, peering through the office windows.

A woman asked for a glass of water, and Mrs. Herndon refused. She did allow three prisoners to use a water closet out in the hall, then changed her mind when Miss Burns asked.

Several hours went by, and some of the women stretched out on the floor to rest. Louise thought it looked none too clean, so she stayed in her seat, wondering how long she could endure the growing discomfort in her bladder.

The door opened, and a big man in a long black coat stepped to the front of the room, where he stood with his arms folded. The number of guards in the hallway had increased. Mrs. Herndon jumped up. "They refuse to give their names, Mr. Whittaker. I've been waiting for you."

The women on the floor sat up, and Mrs. Lewis rose to her feet. "We demand to be treated as political pris--"

"You shut up," Whittaker barked. "I have men here glad to handle you. Seize her!" Two men grabbed Mrs. Lewis by the arms and dragged her out of the room. "And seize her! And her!" Men hauled away Paula Jakobi, a playwright, and slender little Dorothy Day. Miss Burns shouted as her arms were twisted behind her.

Delicate, white-haired Mary Nolan, cried out, "I'll come with you. Don't drag me. I have a lame foot." The men ignored her, but luckily Mrs. Nolan's feet left the ground as they hustled her out. Whittaker still stood in the front of the room, shouting orders.

More guards stomped in, hurling aside chairs that had been emptied. Louise was jerked up from her seat. She smelled stale tobacco breath as two men pulled her toward the door. "Don't resist," she called to Jessie. "There's no need to get hurt."

Outside, the fresh air rushing into her lungs was so welcome, Louise barely noticed the November cold. The darkness was complete except for a light in the window of a low building across the yard, just bright enough to show an American flag flying on the roof. Half-walking, half-dragged, Louise scuffed her boots across the hard ground until she was propelled through a door and down a long central aisle between two rows of cells. The odor of sour bedding and dirty toilets made her want to vomit.

The two men tossed her into a cell, and she skidded across the floor, bruising her shoulder. Jessie and another girl were thrown in after her but landed on the narrow bed. Across the passageway, Miss Day was crying out for help, and Miss Jakobi, struggling with two guards, was trying to get to her. Five men grappled with Miss Burns, who resisted every step. They heaved her into a cell and slammed the door.

At last, boots shuffled away, and relative quiet prevailed. Women wept, groaned, and conversed in low voices. Louise picked herself up and sat gingerly on the bed, holding her shoulder. "Are you all right?" she asked the two girls. Sadie Cutler introduced herself and said she was frightened but unhurt.

"I'm fine," said Jessie. "But what about your shoulder?"

"It'll be all right. Nothing's broken."

"Who's here?" a clear voice rang out. "Miss Lincoln, are you here?"

"Yes," came a reply from down the aisle.

"It's Miss Burns," Jessie said. "Isn't she marvelous? She's not afraid of anything."

The resonant voice continued to shout a roll call. A guard yelled at Miss Burns to shut up. "Where is Mrs. Lewis?" she demanded.

"They've just thrown her in here," someone replied. "She's unconscious."

"If any of you say one more word," a guard threatened, "we'll put you in straitjackets."

Miss Burns went on calling the roll. Two guards handcuffed her wrists to the cell door above her head. Julia Emory, in the cell opposite, raised her hands in the same position and stood there in silent solidarity.

"I'm so cold," Jessie said, keeping her voice low. "And it stinks in here."

The cell had no window and no light. By the corridor lamp, Louise made out an open toilet in the corner, which she gratefully made use of. But there was no handle to flush it. "I was told we have to ask the guards to flush the toilet from outside," she explained to her cellmates.

"Those bullies who dragged us in here?" Miss Cutler said. "I hope never to speak to them in my life."

"Where do we all sleep?" asked Jessie. The flimsy bed and the narrow mattress on the floor were each covered with one gritty blanket.

"I suppose we'll have to take turns sleeping," Louise said. "Or try to jam two of us on the mattress."

"We're friends, so we can take the mattress," Jessie decided. "Miss Cutler, you take the bed."

Exhausted, using their arms for pillows, the three of them managed to fall asleep.

A metal cup clanging against the bars jarred Louise to consciousness, her next sensations being intense thirst and the soreness of her shoulder. She sat up, back and limbs aching from the hard floor. "My mouth's like cotton," Jessie said. Having slept half off the mattress, she rolled onto the floor and then exclaimed, "My God, the filth!" She stood up and brushed her skirts off in the corner, raising a cloud of dust.

"I'm starving," Miss Cutler said. "We haven't eaten since yesterday noon."

"I need a wash." Jessie regarded her grimy hands.

"All right, everyone this way," said a wardress, unlocking the cells one after another. "Mr. Whittaker wants to see you."

They shuffled down the corridor and were allowed to stop at the door, where a large basin of water stood. They took turns dipping a single cup into the bucket to drink, sharing germs freely. Out in the anemic morning light, a lone raven rode the wind against the mottled gray and purple sky. Beyond the fenced yard, crop fields stretched out to a row of trees waving bare branches, snaky and black. A hoarse cry echoed over the yard, and the raven wheeled off.

In the room where the women had sat the day before, the superintendent was waiting. He looked over the rows of anxious faces and pointed to Miss Jakobi, who was on her second visit to Occoquan. "Will you obey prison regulations and do as you're told?"

"No," she replied. "I will not wear the prison uniform, and I demand to be given the rights of political prisoners, as we have been--"

"Then you'll go to the *male* side and be in solitary confinement. Do you change your mind?" "No."

Whittaker gestured to a guard, who grasped her by the arm and led her away. Wardresses herded the rest of the women into another room. The matron came in with three black female prisoners pushing carts piled with clothing. "All right, take off your clothes and put these on," commanded Mrs. Herndon. Louise picked up one of the heavy chemises, made of unbleached muslin the texture of sandpaper. Another cart held drawers of the same material and petticoats of cotton ticking, such as ordinarily was used to cover mattresses. On top, the women were to wear heavy, shapeless gray cotton dresses and dark blue aprons. There were not enough of the thick, clumsy stockings to go around, nor of shoes, which came in two sizes, large and small. Louise was not among those who were allowed to keep their own shoes and stockings due to the shortage. She tried to hide herself as she changed, aware of the watching matron, female guards, and Negro prisoners.

All possessions were taken away with their clothing. The women returned to their cells, still hungry and unwashed. At noon, bowls of thin, greasy pea soup arrived. Some of the women had declared their intention to undertake a hunger strike from the start, but Louise had resolved to eat in the hope that Jessie would eat and keep up her strength. Miss Cutler took a look at the grayish soup and said, "I'd rather starve than eat that."

Louise dipped a spoon into the bowl and conveyed a chunk of pork to her mouth, along with the cloudy broth. She chewed and swallowed, trying not to make a face. "Salty," she said. When she looked back down, a worm had floated to the surface. She picked it out and threw it in the toilet, then forced herself to take another spoonful and then another.

"It smells even worse than it looks," said Jessie. "I'm joining the hunger strike." Louise was torn. Should she eat, just to make sure she had the strength to look after Jessie? Or was it more important to support her friend by fasting as well? She ate half the bowl of soup before giving in to disgust.

In the evening, toast and hot milk were brought, and

although they smelled alluring, Louise had no appetite. Her cellmates refused to take even a taste. That night, intestinal cramps woke Louise repeatedly to sit for long periods of time on the toilet, adding to the ever-present stench. She could see the plate of toast still waiting at the door of the cell in a semicircle of light. A rat was nibbling the crust.

During the daytime, the prisoners sang hymns or made up satirical lyrics to popular tunes, ridiculing President Wilson and joking about the conditions in the prison. In the evening, the pious Helen Bayles, a suff from Maryland, said prayers in a loud voice that all could hear, including the "regular" prisoners housed at the end of the corridor.

"Dear Lord and Father of us all," intoned Miss Bayles on the second evening. "Forgive the matron and trusties for their callous behavior. Forgive Mrs. Herndon for feeding us worms and the most disgusting rotten vegetables sent down from Washington, while the squashes grown on the workhouse land pass by on wagons to be sold elsewhere. Forgive the wardresses for forcing us to shower in front of complete strangers. Forgive Mr. Whittaker for directing men to twist our arms. But if divine justice deems punishment the fit consequence for these tormentors, see to it that they reside in the hottest circle of hell until they repent of their sins. And then, dear God, feel free to keep them there forever, according to thy will. Amen."

The "regulars" laughed harder and longer than the suffs. The matron was incensed.

Much effort went into trying to pass notes among the cells. A few women had hidden pencil stubs and scraps of paper in their cuffs, to be secretly transferred to the prison clothing upon changing. The water pipes running along the backs of the cells had a tiny bit of space around them where they penetrated the walls, just enough room for a slip of paper.

On the third day, after fried chicken and salad had been brought in to tempt the women on hunger strike, Jessie heard a tapping at the pipe. She went to the wall, gave an answering tap, and held out her hand to catch the morsel of paper that came sliding through. "It's from Miss Burns. It says, 'They think there is nothing in our souls above fried chicken.'" They all felt heartened by her mettle.

Jessie went to the other side of the cell to pass the paper onward along the pipe.

The effects of the pea soup seemed to have passed, but Louise felt weakened by the loss of fluids. She was feverish and dizzy, and her skin felt painfully dry, on top of the irritation caused by the coarse clothing. Miss Cutler complained of nausea, while Jessie, although limp with weakness, seemed not to be severely affected by fasting.

That evening, Louise and Jessie were each made to trade places with another suff. "But I must stay with Miss Fulton," Louise protested. "I have to look after her." The guard escorting her snickered and shoved her into a nearby cell, where she sat on the bed, shaking with anxiety. Her new cellmates did their best to comfort her. "Why did they make us move?" she asked.

"It's a way to disorient and upset us," said one of them. "But we're all in it together. Whoever's with your friend will take care of her."

Louise's distress earned her the bed for the night, which made her feel guilty, so she tried to pull herself together. The dizziness had been replaced by a sense of floating, as if her mind had partially detached from her body. The only mercy she found in fasting, besides not having to eat the prison food, was the tendency for sleep to overcome her for much of the day as well as the night.

One morning, when she'd lost track of the passing days, a doctor came into the cell. He barely glanced at the other two women, who were not on hunger strike, but he sat down to take Louise's pulse. That afternoon, she was summoned to Whittaker's office. The wardress who came to fetch her kept tugging at her upper arm, trying to speed her up. The oversized prison shoes felt made of iron as she struggled to lift them on the walk down the corridor and across the yard.

Whittaker greeted her with a broad smile and invited her to sit down. He perched on the edge of his desk, making her shrink back in the chair. "It looks as though your hunger strike has been difficult and painful," he said in a genial voice. "The doctor is worried about your health."

She wanted to say something about the pea soup being the cause of her ill health, but the words refused to take shape on her lips. He put a hand on her shoulder, which made her flinch away. He stood up and walked around to sit behind his desk. "Please tell Mrs. Herndon to come in," he told the wardress. Each time he smiled, Louise fixated on his brownish teeth. When his lips closed, she missed the sense of focus they had given her.

"Where are you from, Miss Kelley?"

She didn't recall giving her name. How had he learned it? She concentrated on the question, thinking it ought to be easy to answer. The two words made their way from her blurred thought to the thick tongue, which was reluctant to move, but she forced it to spit out "New York."

"You're a long way from home. I suppose you miss your people there. Maybe you have a beau, a lover?" The way he said the word "lover," drawing out the letter "l," made her shiver. "You are, I suspect, an attractive woman when you're healthy. I would hate to see your health so ruined that your fellow doesn't want you back. Wouldn't that be a shame?"

She shook her head, trying to clear it. Why was he talking about her beau? The matron arrived, carrying a plate of fried eggs and toast. She held the plate in front of Louise, who almost gagged from the smell. The two yellow eyes staring up at her from the plate made her understand, finally, what Whittaker wanted. Rage funneled its way up from deep in her shrunken belly. The brown teeth, so expectant of cooperation, were showing again. She raised both hands from her lap and struck the bottom of the plate. It flew across the desk and splattered egg yolk across Whittaker's shirt. He swore, batting at his chest. "You are insane! Mrs. Herndon, take this maniac back to her cell. Just wait, Miss Kelley. The doctor will be on his way soon with a straitjacket."

The matron hustled her out, and Louise heard herself laughing. Maybe she was going insane. But once she was back in her cell, the superintendent's threat ballooned in her mind. She was terrified of being confined in a straitjacket, unable to move. How long would he leave her bound up? She curled up on the bed and wept silently, unable to form the words that would tell her worried cellmates what had happened.

No doctor arrived that night. She insisted on taking the mattress on the floor but continued to cry intermittently, helpless to stop, wondering when the straitjacket would come.

The next morning, the doctor walked in with two other men. They took her to a white room and strapped her to a chair while she struggled in panic. When the doctor produced a long rubber tube, she calmed down. It's all right, she thought, they're going to forcibly feed me, and I can survive that.

Miss Burns always fought the procedure, clamping her mouth shut so they had to shove a smaller tube down her nose. Miss Paul did the same. But Louise didn't see any purpose in struggling. She opened her mouth and let the doctor insert the tube. As it slid down her throat, grating against the soft tissue, she gasped, feeling she was going to suffocate. Unable to draw breath around the tube, she began to choke. Her teeth clenched down on the tube. "Oh, stop that now," the doctor said, but her jaw refused to open. Her whole body was shaking, muscles in spasm, as she struggled for breath. "All right then, we'll have to go through the nose. Hold her head still," he said to the two men. He let go of the tube and picked up a narrower one. Her mind swarmed with thoughts of drowning, dying, release.

The tube went up her nostril, and she felt blood trickle over her lips. Furrows of pain dug through her face and followed the tube arcing over and down into her throat. The two men pressed their fingers deeper into her temples and the back of her head. The doctor held up a funnel and began to pour the milk. The liquid slid down the tube and leaked its cold through all the crevices of her throat and head, provoking a repeated throb that echoed in the frantic racing of her heartbeat. The milk took forever to wind its way into the depths of her body, chill and punishing. She couldn't halt the stuttering cry that came through her mouth, as the jaw finally let go. Inkblots of darkness appeared and spread. She gave in to nothingness. ⬤

Bette Ridgeway

If Hillary Won We'd Be At Brunch Now

Paula Rudnick

women walk the streets with signs

ELECTILE DYSFUNCTION
BRAINS ARE THE NEW TITS

their bruises masked with pancake

HELL HATH NO FURY LIKE 157 MILLION WOMEN
SCORNED

they've had enough of curtsies

GODDESSES DON'T SPEAK IN WHISPERS
WE SHALL NOT BE GRABBED

enough being harrassed

CHIN UP, FANGS OUT
MY SHORT SKIRT AND EVERYTHING UNDER IT ARE
MINE, MINE, MINE

they're done faking pleasure

CAN'T BELIEVE WE STILL HAVE TO PROTEST THIS SHIT

done whimpering encouragement

THERE'S SO MUCH WRONG I CAN'T FIT IT ON THIS
SIGN

expert as they are at swallowing

RESPECT EXISTENCE OR EXPECT RESISTANCE
FORWARD NOT BACKWARD

they're ready for the battle

GIRLS JUST WANT TO HAVE **FUN**DAMENTAL RIGHTS

gestated in smiles

RESIST, REST, REPEAT

for a thousand years 🅜🅡

Men Behaving Badly

In Manhattan there's a walking tour
of New York's famous creep men,
buildings where the power-guys
and their young suited wannabes
have preyed on women with a cute behind,
banging, boinking, rogering them,
smashing up against their blazers
to cop a feel of the breasts inside,
scronching, pummeling, groping
despite threat of hashtag me-too swipes,
grabbing, poking, thumping
female underlings who craved a mentor
or who needed work to feed a child.
At 30 Rock - Bill Cosby and Matt Lauer.
Fox News – O'Reilly, Roger Ailes.
CBS – Les Moonves, Charlie Rose.
Too many in one block to name them all.
Tour of the restaurant lechers
offered Tuesdays in the autumn.
Sold out through October. ●

Ralph Lauren Backed the Wrong Horse

Poor Ralph Lauren.
His candidate lost on the evening
of his finest pantsuit.
He was ready to make our country chic again
but he bet on the wrong horse,
bottom dropped from bottom line
as minions headed for the hills
to re-evaluate their options.
Home-grown turquoise of forever young
seems tired now that women have to dress like girls,
thighs and calves in classic skirted S,
lips and tongues clamped tight as knees.
Goodbye packable double-knit,
forgiving of an extra pound or two
when worn with longer jacket.
We and Ralph must weather bitter storms
before our frontier style comes back,
America rebranded as the latest
must-have thing.

Bette Ridgeway

Heroines

Lee Reilly

Where we going?" Rosaleen asked. She was eight. They were headed toward history, at least that's how it felt to Alicia as they threaded through New York City, past people with carts and policemen who didn't look friendly; this was a momentous time, and they were walking in a grand river of human effort, and no one knew how important their mission was.

"A parade!" she said. She didn't say, Of suffragists.

Rosaleen didn't answer. She'd vanished. Where'd she go? Alicia spun around, walked a half block and back again, so many people, it must be the time of day, it was never like this in the Meadows, even Secaucus, even Rutherford. Where was Rosaleen?

There—standing on the other corner, staring at the man with the monkey on his shoulder. A picture she was, in her green dress with her cut-glass green eyes, gazing, about to ask one of her strangely profound questions.

"Rosaleen, come, come, come! And stay with me!"

"Why does the monkey have a chain on his foot?"

"You know Margaret's address? This is a very special parade but if something happens, you know Margaret's address."

"Parade?"

"Yes."

"Why didn't Margaret come?"

So many reasons. At eighteen, Margaret was exceedingly mature. She was *settled*—Mamai's proud term—and married to a butcher who had his own shop in Hell's Kitchen, which didn't sound very settling, Alicia once joked, but no one thought that was funny. Margaret was against women trotting around in flat shoes with signs and shouting. Margaret was also against girls with a sense of humor.

It was starting. Fifty women? Alicia had hoped for more. She'd read about the huge parade last year. She'd been to meetings back in New Jersey, she'd hung signs late at night with a big woman who had a limp and couldn't climb fences. This seemed—small.

"Where's your mother?" A woman wearing white handed her the corner of a banner that was half the width of the street.

Mamai? Here? "I'm *fifteen*."

"And she's—" pointing to Rosaleen.

"She's going to walk right behind me. Very close."

"Where's the parade?" Rosaleen whined.

"You're in the parade," a gray-haired woman said. "Hold my hand."

Why had she brought Rosaleen? As they started to walk and the crowd on the street surged, Alicia tried to remember. Because she wanted Rosaleen to know these things. Because Rosaleen, who talked to birds and wanted to write stories, deserved to know these things. Because she wanted to be Rosaleen's heroine. Because Rosaleen had whined at home, "Can't I go see Margaret? Can't I?" when Margaret was such a dumb brick, and shouldn't be anybody's favorite anything.

A drummer led them. She was wearing pants under her dress. The crowd jeered. "Let a man do a man's work" and "Home wrecker!" and "Street walkers!"

"Why are they shouting about walking on the street?" Rosaleen asked.

When a tall boy tried to grab the drum, the drummer twisted fast and pushed on. Things started flying. Stones. Buckets of water. Parts of things. Policemen watched. Alicia knew about this, the ladies in the meetings had explained it, and Mamai, reading about the beatings, had once said, "If I'd wanted to be roughed up, I for one would have stayed in Ireland," but Alicia didn't realize—she glanced back at Rosaleen. They were fine, the woman in white said. "Stay together," she shouted.

Which they all did until the intersection, where the carts on the other street didn't stop, in fact they sped up, and people—men—dove into the parade, and a horse reared, and policemen waved bobby sticks, and the drummer tripped on a man's foot. Alicia and the woman in white tried to reach the drummer, but the banner was on the ground, tangled up in their legs and the drum, which another boy was trying to steal, and there was blood, and where was Rosaleen?

Alicia scrambled up from the ground, "Rosaleen!"

The gray-haired woman was gone. This was impossible. Alicia pushed past women covering their faces as the crowd surged, and then she climbed the steps of a porch to see more. There was a paddy wagon. The cops were pushing, and women were looking for each other, shouting. One was carrying a flag. A nurse bent over someone on the ground. A woman limped along, carrying a huge doll made to look like Columbia, symbol of America.

Why had she brought Rosaleen?

The paddy wagon moved off. Women were picking up signs, brushing off clothes. She asked everyone. No one had seen the little girl with the cut glass eyes. Alicia stopped circling. Her legs didn't feel like anything.

How could she be lost? Poor Rosaleen.

Stupid to bring her here. Stupid to think she could keep her safe. Stupid to think the world could be safe, she who lived in a place where the water wasn't even safe.

At the police station they said there were no girls. Just ladies of the day. That got a big laugh. She went to the organizer's house. No one was home. Of course not. The woman in white was in jail.

She would have to face Margaret; maybe her butcher husband would take Alicia to all the police stations. How many were there? But if—then how could she face Mamai? How could she face a house without Rosaleen?

She was a block from Margaret's when she saw the giant Columbia, and Rosaleen holding out a note, like a person begging.

"You found me!" Rosaleen yelped. "I knew it. You're so perfect."

Perfect? She'd put Rosaleen in danger for stupid reasons.

"And look what I got, I followed the woman with the doll and she gave it to me and this note and I get to keep her."

"You can't tell anyone where we were."

"Can't I keep Columbia?"

"No."

Rosaleen's eyes filled.

"Yes," Alicia relented. Because Rosaleen wanted it. Because Rosaleen was already talking to it. Because Rosaleen deserved a heroine. ⓜ

Forgivable Offenses

Debra Madaris Efird

Glaring sunshine trades places with shadowy darkness as I drive into the parking deck, fumbling to remove my sunglasses. It's a mild January day, with only a slight chill in the air. People will have to dig deeper than the weather for an excuse to stay home from the Women's March. But from the looks of traffic in the city as I close in on the apartment, no one is risking being left behind. I ease my car into the first available parking spot, turn off the engine, and steel myself for a confrontation with my daughter.

Because, for some reason, Serena and I clash. I don't understand it. The most innocuous topic or activity can lead to conflict. If I say girls like her look good in leggings, she'll say I'm implying she's too skinny. If I tell her I ran into one of her former teachers at the mall, she'll huff that I probably bragged about her too much. But one thing we do seem to agree on is politics, though I am more the extremist than she. So today, though wary, I'm a bit more hopeful for a smooth visit.

I take out my phone and text Serena. She's prickly about me showing up at her door, so unless specifically invited, I meet her in the parking deck. In a few minutes she appears by the car door wearing a fitted pink jacket that flaunts her lean figure, her fresh face framed by a halo of butterscotch hair, her aquamarine eyes luminous in the dim light of the deck. It still startles me that such beauty has sprung from the likes of Ralph and me.

She has a boyfriend now. Garrett. I can't ignore the fact that she's smiling more. The downside is that it's harder for her to carve out time for me.

I pop open the trunk and show her the selection of simple signs I've made supporting a variety of causes: health care, Planned Parenthood, immigrants, LGBT. Serena shakes her head, not wanting to carry one. I grab the Planned Parenthood sign because I know it's her preferred focus, whether or not she wants to trumpet it.

As I close the trunk, she points at my feet.

"Why did you wear those boots?"

I look down at the shoes in question. "Uh, because they're comfortable." A second's pause, and I justify, "We're going to be walking a lot."

"They look like you're expecting sleet," she says. "The sun's out."

As if I haven't noticed. I shrug, deciding to leave it be.

As we walk the short distance into the center city, we find ourselves amidst the throngs on their way to the rally point. Women – and a sprinkling of men – of all shapes, colors, and ages converge on the scene, some pushing strollers.

Ha! That would've never happened in the late 1960's. Few would've risked bringing a child into that capricious environment, when a peaceful protest could turn into a raging riot in a matter of seconds.

I read the signs carried high in the air: Don't Grab This Pussy, Get Your Hands Off My Ovaries, Let's Talk about the Elephant in the Womb.

Whew, the signs of the times have changed as well. But I like their sentiments.

We keep making our way toward the speakers' platform. I want to get close as possible, and Serena yields to my lead. We reach a spot with standing room for two and plant ourselves on the hard concrete. It's a side view, but near enough to the speakers to discern nervousness in their scrabbling with index cards, their licking of lips. As they push through their opening sentences, adrenaline takes over and they wax unflappable. In steady succession, speakers take their places at the mike, building up fervor in the audience.

I've heard these voices before, though the words aren't the same. I've stood in an assembly like this and felt these raw emotions that scream for change.

My mind easily conjures the self-assured young girl I was, ready to take on the world with my fresh unlined face and long straight hair brushing the waist of my faded jeans. Alongside me was a vibrant international student from France, and together we shouted all that was wrong with America. It was November 1969, and we'd joined the massive march in Washington to protest the Vietnam War. It turned out to be the largest anti-war demonstration ever in the history of the United States.

Ah, the lovely Michel. But we hadn't started out as friends.

I met him on the first day of Anthropology class when the professor conducted an experiment which required students to talk to the person beside them about what they noticed first about each other, and then what they noticed second.

"Awkward," I said as I turned to face my partner.

Oh! I hope I have disguised the jolt I felt as I took in his stunning amber eyes, his walnut-colored curls cascading to his shoulders.

"What? You think I am awkward?"

The heavy accent immediately gave away that I was paired with a foreign student.

"No, no. It was a joke. Sort of," I stammered. "I meant, having to do this."

"Oh," he said, and broke into a smile that left me wondering if he modeled for toothpaste ads. "The first thing I noticed about you was your smell."

Uh, really. Did this conversation have to happen?

He continued. "Before class started, I could already smell you." He twitched his nose. "Violets, maybe?"

I allowed myself to feel a small measure of relief. But he could still be toying with me. I knew I should've showered after having sex with Carl last night.

"So, are you always this quiet?" he asked. "I may say the second thing I noticed about you is you are quiet."

I laughed. People who knew me would never say I was quiet. "No," I answered. "First day jitters, I guess." Immediately I realized that would not translate. "It is an unusual assignment, to talk to a stranger," I corrected, with more enunciation and volume than necessary.

"Ah, yes," he said, sotto voce. "But we won't be strangers if we sit in this class together for a whole semester. So what is your name?"

"Diane. And yours?"

"Michel," he answered, a slight cringe creasing his face as he pronounced it.

I smiled. His reaction was an almost inaudible sigh, which I perceived as gratitude that I made no comment on his girly-sounding name.

"One minute," said the professor.

"OK, so the first thing I noticed about you is that you are male," I stated, speaking more naturally. I wanted to say the second thing was that he was too good-looking to also have a sexy French accent. The pause extended, with seconds ticking off the clock pressuring me to respond. "The second thing is that you are white."

He gave me a thin, closed smile.

I regretted it the minute I said it. Because he'd probably already deduced from my accent that I was a Southerner. He'd label me racist. He'd imagine I had a slave cemetery in the backwoods of my rice plantation, for God's sake. But I'd had several Sociology classes and knew that gender and race were usually the first two points that the brain zeroes in on when categorizing information, and that's what came out of my mouth.

The professor called time.

Mom?"

I blink into a familiar face, a beautiful one, but marred by a frown.

"Oh." I hesitate, sensing her impatience with me. "What?"

"See that man over there, the one with the dreads in a ponytail?" she points off to the right. "That's one of the new city council candidates, the one everybody's talking about."

Yes, I've seen him before on the news, usually advocating a far left position that jives exactly with my own politics. Now *he* looks like the kind of guy who would've fit into the 60's scene. He's holding a sign saying, "Nasty Women Get It Done."

"I think he'd get further if he toned it down a bit," Serena says.

I nod to go along. But I'm thinking, crank it up.

Everyone around us is chanting slogans, and we join them: "Show me what democracy looks like. This is what democracy looks like." After a few rounds we go into

"What do we want? Justice. When do we want it? Now." Next it's "Let me hear it, loud and clear. Refugees are welcome here."

I spot the line of portable toilets over to the side and consider a visit. The rally is expected to last half an hour, and then the march will start. Who knows how long the march itself will take, though I'm sure the endpoint will also have facilities. As I calculate my bladder capacity, the crowd hushes as another speaker taps on the mike at the podium.

Serena turns toward me.

"You know what Garrett said when I asked him to come with us today?'

I shake my head. He probably wants to watch football, like Ralph. There's always an NFL game on.

"He said, 'Hell, no.' Not just no, but hell, no."

"Well," I start. I don't know what to say next. Interfering with my daughter's love life has never been beneficial to either of us. Not wanting to ruin the day, I decide to say nothing further.

"I think he thought it would be only women," Serena says, already excusing him. I recognize rationalization immediately, as it's what I do with Ralph. I invited him to come, too, knowing he wouldn't. He's never considered anything remotely political to be his responsibility.

I wait for more, but Serena has shifted her focus to the speaker.

I scan the motley gathering. A middle-aged woman to my left is holding a sign that reads "F*** the President." I suppose she thinks the asterisks make it all right. Though I agree with her message, I look away. I can still remember when the F-word was kept mostly under wraps and not scattered about like confetti on New Year's Eve.

The speaker drones on. There are too many speakers at these things. Everyone just wants to march. I rock forward, balancing on my toes. A trio of African-American girls to my right must feel the same: they're sighing and stamping their feet as if to hurry along the presentation.

The next couple of weeks Michel sat on the opposite side of the room from me. It seemed he came in late so that he could be assured of putting distance between us. Just as well. His enchanting face was a distrac-

tion I didn't need. The professor had already said he didn't give A's. It was a C class, and if you walked on water you might get a B.

But not having to look at Michel didn't block him from my mind because he was always speaking out in class, his melodious accent a sharp contrast to the drone of the professor. He was obviously gunning for a B.

Within a couple of weeks, I started losing interest in Michel. I was busy with my other classes, and Carl and Gregory and Rashid kept vying for my attention, wanting to be the one who warmed my bed at night. It was an electrifying time to be in college, with students not only hyping free love but also beginning to awaken to social justice causes. Proponents of racial equality and women's liberation filled our television screens and radio waves, with the loudest and most spirited attention going to those fighting to end the war in Vietnam.

Mid-semester, not far from the university, a black man was shot in the back by a cop. Multiple witnesses said he had his hands up and was unarmed. The day the officer was cleared, turmoil rocked the community. A group on campus, claiming to be part of the Black Power movement, planned a march to the Capitol building in Raleigh to protest.

With my sense of injustice ramped up, I decided to join them. A Southern girl had to work hard to prove she was trying to shed the racism inherent in her upbringing. I made a poster and approached the mostly black group huddled in the Student Center. And there among the white faces dotting the company was Michel.

"Diane?" he asked, blinking as if seeing a mirage.

"Monsieur Michel," I said, surprised at the delight I felt in seeing him. But apparently it was mutual.

From that point, he came early to Anthropology class and would motion for me to sit by him. We began grabbing lunch after class and then lying around the quad on trampled grass heavily studded with acorns, gazing at the ancient oak canopy above us. We attended free concerts, beer blasts, poetry readings, and the myriad of activities college life offered. Among them, inevitably, was sleeping together.

Quickly I let the other guys fall by the wayside, preferring the company of my lover from Lyon.

I feel the momentum change as the speakers leave the stage and start on the parade route. I glance once more toward the portable toilets but there's not enough time now. The mob is thick and we have to stand still for a couple of minutes before we can fall into place with the other marchers.

Serena is smiling so brightly that it sends a burst of energy into my step. How nice that we can enjoy doing something together that's more meaningful than a pedicure or holiday home tour. And the noise level thwarts conversation, which means fewer opportunities for me to say something that she may misconstrue.

My arms are starting to feel the weight of the sign. As if she senses it, Serena asks if she can hold it for a while. My heart swells with gratefulness as I hand over the sign.

I wonder what details she'll remember of this, her first demonstration march. The exhilaration of the crowd? The resolve of the speakers? Me by her side?

Tall buildings straddle both sides of the street, creating shade which lowers the temperature several notches. With my hands free, I'm able to button the top button of my jacket and rearrange the pink knit cap with its pointy cat ears so that it sits more comfortably. I'm reluctant to call it a pussy hat.

It's an optimistic group, in spite of an incomprehensible election and the resulting inauguration of a man who by any stretch of the imagination is unfit to be President. Even in our collective shock, there is strength in this resistance. I can see hope in the faces of the women around me. Their jaws are set in unified determination; their eyes glitter with vigor and passion.

I sense that everything has changed, including how I'll be spending my retirement years. Previous diversions – volunteering with the Red Cross, meeting friends for lunch, dabbling in art projects – will take a back seat to the effort to regain political power. In my future I see more marches and protests, letters to the editor, frequent contacts with my Congressmen. It will take unflagging effort to fight the inevitable losses coming our way. Today I feel confident to meet the challenge.

Too soon Serena is handing the sign back to me, but at least my arms were able to rest for fifteen minutes or so.

"There's something I need to tell you," she says, her smile gone.

"Oh?" The one thing I'm good at is listening. It's what they paid me for as a school counselor all those years.

Serena glances around to ensure the women behind and beside us are out of earshot. I brace myself.

"I've had a bad Pap smear," she says, her eyes tearing up. "It's probably nothing, but..."

I feel the pang universal to mothers when the health of a child is in question. I place a hand on her arm and steady my voice.

"Oh, honey. I'm so sorry," I say.

I don't mean to say "honey" – it just comes out. Serena hates being called by pet names.

She bites her lip, choosing to ignore the offense.

I continue quickly, asking, "Will you be having a procedure?"

She nods. "Already had it, but I haven't gotten the results back yet."

I pull my arm away as it's difficult to march and hold the sign and give comfort all at once. Declaring everything will be all right pops into my head, though I know it's the wrong thing to say. All but the youngest of children sense the dismissiveness in that line. My mind races through my arsenal of counseling tools, but I feel emotional gridlock. Nothing seems to fit when it's my own child.

Apparently my silence is just what Serena needs, as she goes on.

"Last night Garrett was asking if I've told him the truth about how many sexual partners I've had," she says, ending the sentence with a snort.

I'm on high alert, afraid she'll spew information I'd rather not hear.

"He seems more focused on that than worrying if I could have cancer," she says, wiping her nose with the back of her hand.

I'm ready to grab a butcher knife and mutilate Garrett, chopping off his dick before slashing his throat so that he suffers to the point he begs for death. But I can kill him off in multiple scenarios later. What I need to do at this moment is console Serena.

"I'm here for you when you need to talk. I can go with you to the doctor if you like," I offer, knowing she'll say no.

She shrugs, and says, "Nah. I'll let you know when I

hear."

I touch her arm again. "Thank you for telling me."

Serena looks away from me and picks up the chant the crowd is shouting now: "Fired up. Ready to go."

I muster strength to keep the fear and grief in my heart from spilling over into tears. Not now, with Serena by my side, trying to be brave. I force myself to focus on the topic of my own sexual partners, intimate details I'd never consider sharing with my daughter.

Ralph had come along years after Carl and Gregory and Rashid and Michel. In the intervening time, there had been uncounted trysts as I maxed out on the free love touted by my generation. I'd been lucky, extremely lucky. No unwanted pregnancies, no STDs. Thankfully, the advent of the free love movement occurred well before the age of AIDS.

But of all the dalliances, Michel stands out. He is the one my daydreams occasionally return to, when I allow myself to recall those long ago days before I became burdened by being someone's wife, someone's mother.

T he march in Raleigh had only whetted our appetite for more. The Moratorium March to End the War in Vietnam was coming up on November 15. My own brother, fearing rumors of a draft lottery coming soon, spoke of skipping to Canada. My parents did not want this, for differing reasons. Dad, a WWII veteran, shamed him for trying to "shirk his duty." Mother wept, fearing she'd never see him again. Which we all knew was a possibility, whether draftee or draft dodger.

Women were safe from the draft, but I figured I owed it to my brother and all men to fight against the war in any way I could. Michel, of course, was not at risk, but he shared my fervor. He seemed to know more about America's faults than I did, which only increased my admiration for him.

We stuffed blankets and a few personal items into duffel bags and caught a Trailways bus to DC. It was filled with other young people ready to change the world. Songs from Bob Dylan and Joan Baez echoed through the bus, but the most popular one was "Eve of Destruction," sung by the less familiar Barry McGuire. Marijuana was passed readily along the aisle, the bus driver disregarding the

offense.

Even though we knew the march would be huge, we were not prepared for the spectacle of the masses filling the Mall area. I quickly resigned myself to the fact we wouldn't be able to get anywhere close to the main stage. We joined in the chants circulating around us, yelling our outrage in a unified chorus.

After being gently jostled repeatedly by passersby, it occurred to me how easily we could become separated. I insisted on making a plan for where to meet if that happened. I chose as a landmark the southwest corner of the gigantic Lincoln Memorial reflecting pool. Michel nodded, his eyes focused on the swarm of activity before us.

And inevitably, within hours of arrival, it did happen. We'd headed to the row of portable toilets where we stood in separate lines, as it appeared someone had unofficially designated them male and female. His line moved quickly, whereas I feared I might pee in my pants. When I finally stepped out into the sunlight afterwards, hoping the stench of the toilet had not permeated my skin and clothing, I couldn't spot Michel.

After several minutes of unsuccessful observation, my frustration deepened. I dutifully made my way toward the reflecting pool through the gathering of people. I tired of saying "excuse me" but my Southern upbringing insisted upon it. It was hard not to step on someone's toes or encounter the fiery end of a casually held cigarette or joint. When I finally crossed the expanse of protesters to reach our appointed spot, he wasn't there.

After an hour or so of standing still, I felt panic rising. We'd envisioned building a campfire and lying out under the stars for the night, alongside others. Our return bus trip was not scheduled until late the next morning. Could I sleep out here among strangers? Would we even be allowed to? The police grasped their batons in a fearsome stance, and word spread that they also had tear gas canisters. Like the bus driver, they turned a blind eye to the pot smoking. But that didn't mean they'd let us camp here tonight. Michel and I had both been hopelessly naïve, cocooned in our protective campus world.

But nightfall was hours away. Surely I'd find Michel by then. Speakers were still rallying, though I was too far off to distinguish their words. The crowd murmured that Senator George McGovern was speaking. When Pete

Seeger took the stage and belted out John Lennon's "Give Peace a Chance," everyone could hear that and went wild, singing along. He was followed by some more undecipherable speakers, and then the music of Peter, Paul, and Mary filled the air. Mixed between songs, chants reverberated through the multitude, the most popular being "Hell, no, we won't go!"

While waiting in a long meandering line to grab a hotdog and fries at a concession stand, it occurred to me that maybe Michel had gotten turned around. I wolfed down the food and began making my way to the other three corners of the reflecting pool. I started with the southeast because it wasn't far from the designated site, though there was no clear view from point to point. Dodging all the dense clusters of humanity, I spent nearly an hour walking the full perimeter, which supposedly measured just shy of a mile. No sighting of Michel.

As darkness descended, I parked myself near the southwest corner. Though the Washington Monument was lit up brightly, it was shadowy around the reflecting pool. And chilly. I shivered as I pulled out my blanket and wrapped it around my shoulders. No one had the means to start a campfire even if they'd dared. The police still lined the Mall area, ready to venture into our midst at the slightest provocation.

I found myself being invited to smoke pot by several groups of protesters. At first I declined. But then I decided, to hell with finding Michel, I would join them. The weed was more potent than I was used to, and I got high quickly. All around me were human shapes lying under blankets, moving in the rhythm of sex. I didn't intend to, but I ended up having sex with somebody. He was from New England – Vermont or New Hampshire, I couldn't remember. I never got his name. He had a sleeping bag and we squeezed into it, throwing my blanket over the top.

The sex was not memorable, possibly due to the remorse I felt that I wasn't making love with my Michel under the stars at this pivotal event in the nation's capital. I was thankful for the body heat throughout the night, and for the birth control pill packet in my duffel bag.

The next morning I withdrew myself from the tight quarters of the sleeping bag, relieved that the guy slept on. I grabbed my rumpled blanket, threw it over my shoulders, and trudged to the assigned corner of the reflecting pool.

No Michel. Yesterday that had spiked panic. But now I was too exhausted to care. In a couple of hours I could return to the bus for the long ride home. The bedraggled horde was much thinner, and only a small contingent of police still ringed the area.

After a while, I decided to wander over to the southeast corner. Just in case.

And there, sitting alone, was Michel, huddled in his blanket, his exquisite face marked with a deep frown.

Oh, no. This couldn't have happened.

East and west sound a lot alike in French. But I'd spoken English, of course, and his language skills were better than passable. He couldn't have made such a mistake. And besides, he wasn't at any of the four corners when I'd checked yesterday. If anyone had the right to pout, it was me.

We were hungry, tired, and cold, which easily ratcheted up our anger. I accused him of wandering off with some beautiful girl – or several – and forgetting about me. He wouldn't admit it, but I knew twenty-year-olds rarely turned down sex; I obviously hadn't. The hickeys on my neck sold me out, in case he couldn't smell the scent of the other man on my hair and skin.

I could not let go of my resentment that our special time at this epic event had turned into a bust. And it was all his fault. His inattention to detail had led us to lose focus on the war protest – the reason we'd come. Now we were caught in our own private skirmish. At first Michel kept shaking his head, dodging blame. But then he shrugged it off as if he didn't care. And why should he care – about any of this? It wasn't *his* country killing off *his* brothers. All the way home on the bus we barely spoke, sulking like little kids.

Shortly after our return to campus, I thought things would get back to normal. Both of us were guilty of pardonable offenses. But something was off. I'd ask him to meet for lunch; he'd say he was busy. When he invited me over to his room, it was just for sex. We didn't talk. There was no spirited banter, no lighthearted comparisons of his country and mine. By semester's end, we'd slipped further and further down each other's list.

We lost each other there in DC, in more ways than one.

My reverie is interrupted by a shift in the atmosphere, a harsh cacophony of voices coming from the next intersection. As we move closer, I see counter-protesters running on the sidewalk toward the corner, waving signs saying "Repent!" while holding Bibles over their heads. I hear them yelling the messages on their signs: "Abortion is Murder" and "Homosexuality is an Abomination."

Bystanders have been non-confrontational to this point. The marchers around me are looking at one another with widened eyes, as if unsure how to react. A few are shouting back at the pinched faces of the pious, ordering them to go home or get lost. One marcher cries, "Go rain on someone else's parade." Another yells, "Love is the answer."

I shudder at these genteel responses. Don't these women know how to fight back? Why aren't they angrier?

Heat surges through my body as I tally the injuries smoldering within: the enduring bitterness that Michel and I couldn't work things out, the fresh fury towards Garrett for questioning Serena's sexual experience, the unexpected rage toward a God who would inflict my daughter with a bad Pap smear.

I'll show these marchers how to respond.

I push my sign into Serena's hands, avoiding eye contact which might reveal her disapproval. As I do so, I realize I'm resentful of her as well. For continually creating an atmosphere in which I doubt myself and feel I must walk on eggshells.

My heart goes rat-a-tat, rat-a-tat, as clarity dawns: ultimately I'm mad at myself. For allowing her this power over me. For not laying claim to my own voice, strong and passionate.

Energy fueled by anger propels me forward. I storm over to a woman holding a "Repent!" sign and yank it from her hands. She has liver spots and wrinkles on her face; we're probably about the same age. Her eyebrows arch and her mouth hangs open as she steps back. I flip the sign so that its commanding word is facing her and hoist it high in the air.

"No, *you* repent! *You* repent!" I shout and motion towards her group. "*You* repent for being a part of *this* disgrace!"

I hear a few loud yeahs coming from behind me, followed up with a small chorus of marchers repeating, "*You* repent! *You* repent!"

In the midst of the religious protesters I see a parting as two policemen head over. I thrust the sign toward the woman.

"Here, take back your ridiculous sign."

My hands are shaking and my stomach is turning somersaults, but I pause in front of her in case the cops want to arrest me. But they're not interested in the conflict when they see that we are just two old ladies. No one is coming to blows here. The officers simply urge us marchers to keep moving, saying they don't want any bottlenecks.

I fall back into place with Serena, whose face is flushed. From shock? Embarrassment? Anger? I don't know because she says nothing.

All around me the crowd starts to roar the chant, "My body, my choice!" I remove my sign from Serena's arms and hold both it and my head high as we continue down the street.

A few blocks later Serena breaks the silence with a spark in her eyes and a smile tugging at her lips. "Well, Mom, it looks like we made it. And no one got arrested." She motions ahead to the rally endpoint.

I see no need to respond. I am content with this acknowledgment.

Marchers peel off the street toward the park, mingling with those who have already completed the route. Immediately I notice how much kinder the grass is underfoot than asphalt, and I realize how tired I am. The confrontation with the counter-protester has taken something out of me. And I'm weighed down by the more serious concern of the day: Serena's health news. Yet it's reassuring in a sense, as it appears I'm still needed by this daughter of mine. Female problems unite women in a way men can never understand.

I head straight toward the portable toilets while she gets in a line to buy us drinks. But not before designating a very specific meeting point: the street sign at the corner of Third and Stonewall, in front of Panera.

When I return, she hands me a Coke. She has bought a coffee for herself, a much more sensible choice when outside in January. But she knows what I like.

As we drink, my brain is still tracking memories of Michel and our lost relationship. I start to tell her that maybe

Garrett's reaction to her Pap smear scare is normal, maybe he's as frightened as she is. Maybe he cares more about her than he can admit. That she should give him a little more time to process this jolt. That people striking out against each other in anger and blame may end something prematurely, something that is actually worth saving.

I take a deep breath, but before I can say anything, her cell rings. It's Garrett, she mouths to me. Her voice is guarded as she steps away to talk to him. She positions herself by a row of camellia bushes, the pink blooms matching the hats of women all around. I watch my daughter from a distance. She cannot stay still; she is rocking back and forth from heel to toe. She twists to the left and then to the right, and I catch a glimpse of her animated face. She is absolutely beaming when she slides the phone into her jacket pocket. As she approaches me she adjusts her face into a more stoic expression, the hint of a Mona Lisa smile on her lips.

"Garrett is on his way to meet us. He's coming from Fourth Street, so it'll take him a few minutes." She takes a long swig of her coffee and then turns slightly to the side to avert her eyes.

My heart jumps with her words, but I can play at nonchalance myself.

"Well, that's a step forward," I say, banishing any trace of enthusiasm from my voice.

The sun is unblocked here in this open space, and its warm rays embrace us, welcome us. In silence we watch the mass of people still making their way towards us, ready to reach the oasis of the park. There is time to say those things in Garrett's defense, but I'm not sure that I need to.

In a few minutes he emerges from the throng.

He's carrying a sign!

I squint to read "A Woman's Place is in the Resistance." Serena breaks into a smile so vivid it could not possibly be suppressed.

He's rallying late, but not too late. A forgivable offense.

Someone brushes me and I catch the faint scent of violets. I turn to follow the fragrance, but it's lost in the crowd. ◉

Bette Ridgeway

Bette Ridgeway

Matters of Credit

Nancy Johnson

A hand jolts her shoulder, she opens her eyes and he's standing there beside the bed, all blue suit and attitude, looking down on her.

"What's wrong with you these days?"

She shakes the dreamy images from her mind, looks over to the clock radio, brown and laminated on the end table. "I'm sorry, I must've slept in. Be right with you."

"You're too late. Got my own breakfast. Again."

She pulls the covers back, sits at attention on the edge of the bed. He turns to the dresser mirror and runs his fingers through Brylcreemed hair, his reflection fixed on her.

"Really, what do you do all day?"

She peers down at her polished toenails sunk in the pink, plush pile.

"Why don't you at least get out and pay that bill today?" His mirror image holds its gaze.

"Okay." She hangs her head until he finally turns away.

"I'll be home on time."

The front door clicks shut and her shoulders slump. *What do I do all day?*

She slides her painted toes into fluffy slippers and shuffles around the bungalow, pondering his question. The appliances gleam, the countertops are clear, the pantry is full and the air is Florient-fresh. Just like yesterday. Nothing has changed in the night, or the night before, or in the dozens of nights before that.

They say she should be happy, grateful. What more could a girl want? But, she can't put her finger on it. There's something in her, smoldering. And every now and again a flicker. She feels like getting mad, or even. But for what?

She shakes her head, grabs her new Hoover vacuum, the one he gave her last anniversary, and starts her routine. By early afternoon that's it, nothing left to do. She looks in the mirror.

He's right. I need to get out.

Her words are firm as she faces off against the little man behind the credit counter at Worster's department store. "Wrong? What could possibly be wrong?"

She looks at his pinstripe suit. Shiny and worn. Where does he get off with this haughty stance? And that puffy bowtie cinching that frayed collar at his throat looks like it's damaged his neck. Why else would his chin be tilted upward in an angle that lets such a small man look down his nose at her?

"I beg your pardon." He clears his throat, adjusts the knot in his tie and points a spindly finger to the signature line on the cheque in front of her. "Please sign here, Mrs. Dinwiddie."

She moves the pen, but it happens again. There are ample funds in the account to cover this bill. The date is right, June 5, 1965, and the amount, seventy-six dollars and twenty-eight cents, payable to Worsters. But when she finishes writing, "Mrs.," it's like the wrong end of a magnet repels her hand from the paper. Her sizeable, wedding diamond glints in the light as her hand trembles and hovers above where she needs to sign her name.

"Are you certain there is nothing wrong?" He straightens his posture, folds his hands on the counter and looks right at her. "Perhaps you would like to pay in installments, Madame?" Now his nose seems to tilt even further skyward.

She looks down at his bowtie. Maybe she could tighten it just a notch.

"I told you everything is fine." This time her voice sounds shrill even to her and, in the far recesses of her mind, she hears her English professor, "The lady doth protest too much." She takes a deep breath and sticks the pen back in its scabbard bolted between them on the counter. "I just remembered something. I'll be back."

She turns on her spiked heel away from the credit office, out to the retail area. Her jaw is clenched as she marches away and every muscle stays taut until she hears a familiar creak in the plank floor beneath her. The underwear department. Not much has changed in the half decade since she worked here to pay her tuition. Same floor, and the mixed scent of new fabric and dusty boxes still hangs in the air. Her body slackens.

A young clerk follows behind meandering customers, restoring order to row upon row of items neatly lined up on waist-height display counters. Just like she did all those countless nights, mindlessly arranging colourless brassieres and hefty underpants, daydreaming or pondering the day's Shakespeare or Cervantes lecture. Now, as she gazes once again over the mounds of white cotton, her mind drifts to some fleecy sheep in a seventeenth century pastoral setting...

> ... "Sweet light of my life, I kneel before thee and pledge thee my troth." The scent of garlic wafts up from the handsome shepherd bowed in reverence before her.
> "Foolish fellow. I want for nothing. I have my own flock, a room of my own in yon woods. What temptation could possibly entice me to renounce such wealth and the pleasing companionship of shepherdesses for the certain bondage of matrimony?" She stands, hands on hip bones, looking down on the wretched soul, his face awash in misery. His pleading eyes meet hers and...

"You look like you could use some help."

She starts at the voice behind her, takes her hands from hers hips and reels around to face the young clerk.

"No, no, I feel perfectly fine," but the girl's brown eyes stare at her in a way that suggests the young woman is not convinced.

"I mean help with finding your size." The clerk's brow crinkles beneath her short bangs.

"Really, I'm just looking, thank you," and she scurries away with her head down hoping to hide the annoying blush singeing her cheeks.

When she figures she's out of eyeshot, she stops in a far corner of the department, heaves a what-the-hell-am-I doing sigh and looks about. The big, pale, granny garments that dominated the collection are still here. But now there are youthful bikini bottoms and matching sets of bras and panties in black and even red? In Mr. Worster's department store? What happened to all his rules? That stern list in the big, wooden frame looming above the punch clock? It was rule number six that said female staff were not to wear red. She remembers the night when a senior girl explained that rules like numbers six and nine, that forbade men and women from eating together, arose from old man Worster's sexual repression. That's why the males and females had to eat in separate lunchrooms. According to her co-worker, Mr. Worster thought women chewing in public or wearing red were erotic. And now red underwear?

She shakes her head, turns back to the section with the sensible, cotton under-things and stops beneath a limbless, lifeless torso on the display shelf above rows of practical briefs. She picks through the stock for a pair her size, raises it to the light and thinks of the starched apron she'll wear tonight, like every night, when she greets her husband at the door with his martini.

It's been the same thing ever since they married. Dusting and tidying and putting dinner on the same plates on the same table at the same time every night. Always meat or fish, potatoes and a vegetable or two, served at 6:00 sharp, just as he likes. What if she changed their routine, if only just slightly...

> ... She hooks her new electric can opener onto the Alpo tin and it spins around until the lid springs off, releasing the trapped aroma of mashed liver. She scoops the contents into the bowl, squeezes on some ketchup, and cracks an egg over it all. She sprinkles onion soup powder on top then squishes everything together with a fork from the stainless steel utensils he gave her for Christmas. When it's all well-blended she transfers the mixture into the Teflon loaf pan from the set he gave her for her birthday, puts it in the oven and sets the temperature. A noise. She flings a tea towel over the empty can and swings around just in time to face him.
> "You're home early."

"Meeting got cancelled. What's for dinner?"
"It's Thursday. So, meatloaf. Ok?"
"Sure, sounds good."
She turns away just as the corners of her mouth twist upward ...

"What's so funny, Mrs.?" A pimply stock boy looks at her quizzically as he passes by carrying a large box.

"Nothing, nothing at all." She lowers her head hoping he won't see the burn that's tingeing her face. She tosses the bland garment back on the shelf and the young fellow disappears into the distance. *What is the matter with me?*

She scans all about and checks over both shoulders. No one's looking. She skulks back to the corner with the sexy lingerie and closes in on the blonde, shapely mannequin that models a crimson, push-up bra and matching, bikini panties. With furtive glances to each side, like a thief about to take something, she reaches into the collection of red underthings. She caresses one delicate pair and raises it to her face. So soft, so silky. She strokes her cheek with the cool satin and purrs when she thinks of how especially luxurious it would feel against her concealed parts. What if she traded her uninspiring unmentionables for these scarlet temptations? Dare she alter the regular menu of their weekly sex life? She closes her eyes...

... The mantel clock chimes. She peeps over her Harlequin at him in his wing back chair in the corner. He tucks his pipe in his shirt pocket, just like every night at ten, then rises, crosses the living room and leans down over her. The scent of amphora tobacco fills her nostrils. "I'm ready for bed," he says and gives her a peck on the cheek, a signal as reliable as a traffic light. A peck means he'll read for fifteen minutes, roll over and fall asleep like every weeknight. On Saturday and sometimes Sunday too, he kisses her on the lips, the signal they can make love. She knows every move he'll use, every sound he'll utter, how long it will take.

He leaves the room and she heads for the bathroom. In moments she emerges in nothing but a cherry red g-string and a feather boa that snakes around her long neck and tumbles down, barely concealing her bountiful breasts.

"Oscarrrr," she growls from the doorway. He raises his head from the pillow, eyes stretched open to their limit. She struts in stilettos toward him.
"But it's not the weekend," he pants.
"Your point?" she croons in a Mae West voice as she twirls the tail of the boa.
"But we've never..."...

"Hey lady, watch out." A teenager ducks out of the way of her whirling purse.

"I'm sorry. . ." The wave of heat erupting from her chest flushes across her face.

She looks at her watch. He'll be home soon and expect dinner.

She lowers her head and charges back to the credit office, stops in front of the snippy clerk and slaps her cheque book on the counter between them. She grits her teeth and grabs the pen. She writes, "Worsters," and forges on. The ballpoint glides across the paper until she finishes writing, "Mrs.." The tremor resumes. Again, her hand suspends in the air above the paper.

Her eyes twitch. She looks from hand to pen to cheque and back. Then the words at the top corner catch her eye. "Mrs. Oscar Dinwiddie, 123 Oak..." More twitches. Slowly she re-reads. This time the letters in the given name pop out like figures in a shadow box: Mrs. OSCAR Dinwiddie. Her heart races, breaths grow rapid. The pen moves on its own, like the pointer of a Ouija board, straight up to the printed information, until...a forceful swipe! The mighty weapon drives a horizontal stake through the heart of that name. ~~OSCAR~~! One last time her hand returns to the blank spot that waits for her signature. This time it writes with a flourish.

Breathing relaxed and pulse slowed to normal she hands the signed cheque to the credit officer.

"But, Madame, this is highly unusual."

She juts her chin forward. "How so?"

He rolls his eyes. "I'm certain you understand, Madame, it is customary for a wife to use her husband's name in matters of credit."

"Do I look like an Oscar to you?" She throws back her shoulders and thrusts her ample bosom toward him.

He gapes at her chest. "N-n-no, M-m-madame."

"My name is Mildred. Mrs. MILDRED Dinwiddie." She grows an inch in an instant as her spine straightens to its maximum length. "This is *my* account. Do you want me to pay it or not?" She glares down at him and stabs the pen back in its sheath.

"Of course," his voice crackles. His hand quivers as he gives her a receipt.

Head high, Mrs. MILDRED Dinwiddie, tucks the paper in her purse, turns away from the little man and sashays back to the red, matching set in Mr. Worster's lingerie department. She wonders how it might look under her starched apron. She might paint her toenails red and order takeout tonight. She likes Chinese. She's not sure about Oscar. But it doesn't matter. Tonight, around 6:30 or so, she will order Chinese. And in the far recesses of her mind she hears her English professor one last time, "Graze on my lips; and if those hills be dry, stray lower, where the pleasant fountains lie." Ⓜ

Stepping Out on Derby Day

Virginia Betts

The moment before I stepped out,
Time arrested;
I saw the future played out before me
like a news reel;
like the life I would not live.

All sound stopped.
There was no chattering crowd,
jostling for a space against the fence.
I did not hear
crashing iron hooves,
or feel the ground's vibration
rise up through my feet,
and into my chest
to compete with my dancing heart,
and the sound of blood pounding
through my swimming head.

The air sizzled with static,
as if earth were anticipating;
bracing for impact.
There was no question
of waiting;
we were meant to meet-
the horse and I-
on this unexpected battlefield.

Not a drawn-out fight;
an almighty explosion of light
and sound, thundering down,
to plough me to the ground,
its rippling body tearing
into mine.

One small step for woman
to change the course of time.

Natasha

Coroner rules Avon and Wiltshire trust failed in the care of Natasha Abrahart

Neglect by a mental health trust contributed to the suicide of a Bristol University student with severe social anxiety who was found dead on the day she was due to take part in a "terrifying" oral test, a coroner has ruled. After the inquest, Abrahart's parents also blamed the university, claiming it failed to put in place measures to help their daughter even though staff knew for six months that she was struggling.

They wonder what her future would have been.
Two grey warriors for justice
carry their evidence in a plastic bag,
fight for what is right;
consumed by pain's white heat,
trying to reconcile love with loss.

Torments them, the unwritten script:
Scientist; Woman; Mother? Wife?
An empty hole;
An unlived life.

Grief meets Anger;
unravelling tangles,
uncovering the scandal
of how she asked for help,
which did not come.

Even justice stings;
They scarcely stand, diminished.
Her room a mausoleum of dust, untouched.
In the corner, a pink teddy bear;
a cello with a broken string. 🅜

Dysmorphic

Nobody hates me more than
my own worst enemy.
Can't even cry;
don't want to say.

My face in the back of a spoon,
upside-down, reflected back, distorted,
like a clownish cartoon.
Huge-eyed fly can't settle.

Magnified five times,
I disappear.
Examine fine lines
that turn into crevices
hiding secrets.

Like thin, grey elastic,
I am over-washed;
over-stretched.
Tiny fibres spring loose and fray,
Pinging coils like serpent tongues.

The mirror sends back distress signals,
warping flesh into dough,
spilling out,
when only yesterday,
bones jutted like
splayed rudders.

No anchor. Sharp thought assaulted,
whip-lashed by bright white spikes.
Bed of nails, grown numb,
So over-used.

Perhaps hide, wrapped within
my thick, black habit,
While this disease

brings me to my knees.

Silence the swarming
crackle of brain on fire,
dragging disorder into chaos.

One last black look
before I head off. ⬤

Desco Drive

Kay Smith-Blum

Historical Note

In 1924, a case came before the Supreme Court of Texas for which all of the sitting justices had a conflict of interest. The justices were all members of the Woodmen of the World (WOW), an organization akin to the Rotary Clubs of today and the defendant in the case. Progressive Texas Governor, Patrick Neff, suggested drafting female attorneys.

The legislature, balking at the idea of women, set a requirement that any appointee must have practiced law in the state of Texas for a minimum of seven years. At the time, less than two dozen women were licensed to practice. Neff initially appointed three extraordinary women, all glass ceiling breakers in a variety of arenas and all suffragettes.

Governor Neff appointed Hortense Sparks Ward, the first woman to pass the Texas State bar exam in 1910 and the first woman to practice before the United States Supreme Court, as chief justice of the special all-female Supreme Court of Texas. Nellie Gray Robertson had worked her way through college and law school. In the fall of 1918, she became the state's first female county/district attorney at age twenty-four despite the fact women could not yet vote in general elections. Though tapped for the special court, Nellie was shy of the seven-year requirement by three months.

Edith Therrel Wilmans, admitted to the Texas bar in 1918, helped organize the Dallas Equal Suffrage Association in 1914 and was the first woman to be elected to a state-level position in Texas. But she, too, resigned her appointment because she lacked two months of the requisite seven years. It is generally thought that Wilmans recommended her longtime colleague Hattie Leah Henenberg to Governor Neff. Born to Hungarian Jew immigrants, Henenberg passed the bar in 1916. A lifelong activist for women's rights, Henenberg also founded the Texas Bar Association's Legal Aide Bureau (now Legal Aide of NW Texas).

Neff named the last appointee, Ruth Virginia Brazzil, to the now derisively nicknamed Petticoat Court just twenty-four hours before the court convened.

Chief Justice Cureton administered the oath of office to the final three appointees. No women were among the spectators at the ceremony. Laughter ensued when each woman affirmed under oath that they had never participated in a duel. Afterwards, the clerk of the court reportedly refused to play nursemaid to a female court and declared he would go fishing. *The New York Times*, however, heralded the occasion on January 8, 1925, with a headline that read:

"Supreme Court of Women, First Such Body in the Country Meets in Texas Today"

February 1967

The small Tudor cottage, marooned on the block of sprawling fifties ramblers, segregated itself with a yard thrice the size of its footprint. Hattie rapped on its door. The door swung open and her irritation propelled her forward. She caught herself on the doorframe and rocked back, taking a stand next to a pot of dormant chrysanthemums. Tawny curls bounced across the blue eyes that greeted her.

Hattie cranked her arm at a right angle, like a traffic cop, pointing to the truck behind her. "You can't park there." The battered hulk of iron, parked cattywampus over the tandem driveways, prevented Hattie from exiting her own.

"I'm sorry. Who are you?" The girl buried her hands against the morning chill in her SMU sweatshirt that hung askew over her flannel night gown. She shifted in her stance, centering her body in the door frame, creating a solid target for Hattie's wrath.

"I'm your inconvenienced next door neighbor." Hattie tugged at her blazer, indicating her car with a backwards nod. "The one who cannot get out of her own driveway because of that excuse for a truck."

The girl registered the crux of the matter and said it again. "I'm sorry. I think my boyfriend didn't quite make our drive last night. We got in really late."

"I'm not inquiring into your dating history. I simply need to depart my property without mowing down my garden." She had nurtured those Georgian bushes through a particularly disastrous winter and had no intention of endangering them now. Hattie put her hands on her hips. "Do you have the keys?"

The girl cast a glance behind her. Over her shoulder, a chair drifted from its assigned spot at the dining room table. Dirty dishes spread from the table to the kitchen counter. A faint scent of ginger pierced the air.

"It's Jay's truck. He's still sleeping."

Hattie snorted her impatience. "I didn't ask whose keys they were. I asked if you had them." Decades of courtroom face offs with deadbeat dads had honed Hattie's ability to stay on point. "My sister will be late for her doctor's appointment if you continue to ramble on."

The girl backed into the room. "Just a minute." She lifted a jacket, running her hands through its pockets, then a pair of jeans. A jangle announced a find. Jay remained missing.

"Come on. Time is of the essence." Hattie retraced the front walk at a clipped pace. Mildred peered through the windshield of their Impala.

The girl stepped outside. "I hope it will start. It's been persnickety this week."

Hattie swallowed a smile. Most of the younger generation did not use such adjectives. Hattie tallied this second telltale sign of rural southern roots with the almost indiscernible drawl. Hattie rounded the truck's rear end, noting with a self-satisfied nod that the license plate read Mississippi. Two more strides put her next to her own driver's door.

The girl stepped onto the running board of the truck. The starter whirred without ignition. Hattie approached the passenger side of the truck.

She directed through the open window. "Put it in neutral and release the clutch." The girl cast her a doubtful look. "Young lady, do as I say. You're on a flat surface." The girl repositioned the gearshift and lifted her left knee. "OK, push the clutch all the way down, very slowly, then turn it over." A distinctive squeal resounded. The engine sputtered into life.

The transmission growled along with Hattie. "Your clutch is going. Keep it down and put the gear in reverse." The old Ford pickup on their farm in Ennis had required the same soft touch. "Now, let it out, slow as you can, as you feed the gas." Hattie stepped away. "Well, what are you waiting for?"

The bad clutch screamed its way to the street. Hattie slid into her driver's seat, winked at her sister and steered her own car out of the driveway. Without a backward glance, she headed east on Desco Drive.

The Saturday mid-morning sunlight pawed across the lawn taking the rest of the dew in its grasp. The temperature would climb soon and Hattie wanted to beat it. She hefted the soil-filled wheel barrow down the drive, reluctant to admit she was getting too old for this kind of thing.

The two sisters were just eleven months apart, middle rungs left in a ladder of six siblings. Mildred's two grown daughters had moved east long before Harry, Mildred's husband, died last year. Hattie, the sole family member left in town, rented out her home and moved in with Mildred. This small patch of dirt offered little respite from days now consumed by caring for her sister.

A whiff of Ivory soap played across the hedge row. Hattie's new neighbor stood opposite the azaleas. The young woman's curls were twisted up in a knot revealing a heart-shaped face with fine features. Her cotton plaid shirt topped jeans cinched with a braided tie.

"Want some help?"

Hattie measured up the offer. Skin and bones as her mother used to say, but the rolled-up sleeves revealed muscular forearms likely capable of delivering a punch.

"It depends. Any good with a shovel?"

The girl's mouth broadened into a smile. "I've used one a time or two." Hattie sneezed, her allergies kicking in. "Bless you."

Hattie ignored the girl's auto-blessing and pointed to

the structure beyond the carport. "In there. Grab a shovel for each of us." The girl entered the shed and emerged double-fisted for Hattie's review. "These azaleas had a tough time this winter. Too many freezes for their soul." The girl handed one shovel to Hattie. Hattie pointed to the bushes. "We need to turn the soil before we mix in the new."

The girl nodded, pointed her shovel at the ground and jumped with both feet onto its step, burying it. Springing off, she leveraged the dirt up and out, dumping it to the side. She repeated the action as she spoke.

"My mama taught me to use my whole self when I need strength."

Hattie eyed the girl. "A reasonable approach to any problem. Your mother sounds like a logical woman."

"Yes, ma'am. That she was." The girl kept her eyes on the ground, revealing no emotion over the statement intimating her mama's death.

Hattie dug a bit, then dropped to her knees, sorting out the weeds. She refused to use those new weed killers. Bad for the soil, bad for the gardener. A lawn mower hummed across the street. Hattie grimaced, freshly mown lawns being a source of nasal torture.

Hattie pulled out her handkerchief and gave her nose a good blow. "Are you attending SMU?" The girl cocked her head. "Your sweatshirt, the other morning."

"Yes, ma'am. Summer semester, too. Trying to graduate early." The girl shrugged the information off as no big deal.

Hattie admired hard work. She perched on her heels. "I'm Hattie. What's your name?"

The girl kept her head to her task as she responded. "I'm Grace." She jumped again on her shovel unearthing river stone, remnants from the creek rerouted to enable development.

Hattie slipped a thin, wafer-like stone into her pocket. "Shouldn't you be studying for finals?" Hattie still guest lectured at her alma mater. Final testing periods began in early May.

"I needed a break. Saw you out here." The girl shrugged again. "I like digging in the dirt."

Hattie turned the last of her side of soil and rotated her aching wrists before scooping a shovel-full of compost onto the turned earth.

The girl watched it land. "Is there a bucket in the shed?" Resourceful. Hattie nodded, burying her inner smile. The girl took the lap to the shed again, returning with both a bucket and a hoe. She handed Hattie the hoe. "I'll dump. You mix."

She gathered compost into the bucket and dumped. Hattie raked the hoe back and forth, careful not to bury the trunks of the bushes. The girl moved to the other side. Hattie stretched into a partial backbend. A welcome cloud veiled the sun.

Grace upended the wheelbarrow, shook out the last bit of compost and guided the wheelbarrow into the shed. She returned to admire their handiwork, the garden separating them to their sides.

"Well, I better get back to it." Grace turned toward her house.

Hattie's question followed the girl's back. "What subject are you studying?"

The girl squinted into the sunshine. "A prelaw requisite. Constitutional law, II. Rights."

Hattie slipped her hand inside her pocket and rubbed the stone. "Ah," Hattie said, "so you want to be a lawyer."

"I think so." The girl pulled open her door with one hand and deadheaded a dianthus with the other.

The effortless multi-tasking, the solidity of her stance, the uplifted chin, all so familiar it made Hattie blink. "Well, they won't just hand you the degree." Hattie let the stone slip back down into her pocket. "Best you know it's what you want before you waste any more effort."

The girl lowered her chin, a glint in her eye. "Yes, ma'am."

H attie bent over to grab a grocery sack from the Impala's back seat, exhaling an expletive as an apple rolled out of reach.

"Let me help you with those." Mabel, her across-the-street neighbor, stood on the sidewalk. A leash extended from her hand to her miniature poodle.

"Oh hello, Mabel. The bag boy got a bit carried away trying to save on sacks. All of these are tipsy with produce." Another apple rolled out of reach as Hattie hefted a second bag. Hattie whispered an exasperated, "Damn."

Mabel lassoed her poodle to the porch post, picked up

the bag Hattie had set on the driveway and followed her to the front porch. "Have you met your new neighbor?" Mabel cocked her head toward Grace's side of the driveway.

Hattie plopped her sack on the porch swing and relieved Mabel of hers. "Yes, just after she moved in." Hattie placed the second bag next to the first and waited for it.

"So, you know." Mabel's scowl included a familiar judgment.

While Jewish homes intermingled with Protestants and Catholics in the north Dallas suburb, long-established prejudices hovered all around. "Know what exactly, Mabel?"

Mabel headed back to Hattie's car. Hattie bent down to loosen the poodle's leash.

Mabel paused next to the Impala. "That she's seeing a Negro."

Hattie circumvented Mabel, extracted a bag from the back seat and shoved it with a fair amount of force into Mabel's arms.

Mabel prattled on. "My husband thinks the management company didn't know or they never would have leased to her."

Hattie snatched at the last bag and the errant apple and kicked the door closed with her foot. Sidestepping Mabel, Hattie tossed her response over her shoulder.

"What makes you think that?" Hattie hoisted her bag onto the porch swing and regarded her neighbor with a long cool look and a crease of a smile. The poodle edged toward the street.

"That colored man she sees, he can't live here. And they are definitely not married, God forbid. Neither wears a ring." Mabel snorted showing her disgust for Grace's relationship on multiple levels.

Hattie relieved Mabel of her grocery bag. "Most folks use the term 'black' these days. Your vocabulary is outdated, as is your knowledge of housing laws in Dallas."

A squirrel bounded across the street with Mabel's poodle in pursuit.

"Oh dear, your dog is loose."

"How in the world?" Mabel's question rose and fell as she tore off after her pet.

Hattie turned her back on the scene. She lifted her hand to the mezuzah in the doorframe and closed her eyes. The value of humility eluded her along with the patience she sought. A car screeched. Yelps erupted. Hattie opened her eyes. The poodle was fine. Hattie began ferrying grocery bags inside.

Back to back episodes left most of Mildred's left side limp. Every muscle in Hattie's seventy-one-year-old body protested lowering her sister into bed. She straightened the twists in Mildred's blue nightgown. A plethora of prophetic oceanic shades filled Mildred's closet, stormy to clear sailing. Hattie propped a second pillow behind Mildred's back. Though many of her muscles had been taken to their bare minimums, her eyes had not been affected. Her doctor repeatedly expressed the luck of that.

Hattie handed Mildred her novel and teased. "Not exactly a classic."

Mildred retrieved a chalky-green mint out of her bedside jar and popped her sister in the chest. "Take that, you hypocrite. I've seen you enraptured more than once by a romance magazine." Mildred's mischievous smile refused to appear on the left side. "And, I left my story mid-embrace last night. Who knows where that might lead?"

Hattie tucked an errant strand of hair behind Mildred's ear, searching her sibling's eyes. "Are you sure you're OK?"

"Look at it this way. Half of me is already asleep." Mildred grinned her lopsided grin. "My story will take me the rest of the way."

Hattie left the door slightly ajar. She scanned the shelves in the library full of law books, purposely out of reach, mourning the loss of Perry Mason, the decade-long whodunit starring her favorite television lawyer. How the network could have canceled such an intelligent series boggled. She plucked a hardback off the shelf and poured a conciliatory glass of sherry. She settled into the living room easy chair and opened the well-worn Jane Austen tale to page one.

Hattie started awake to loud voices. The reading light held off the dark. A last sip of sherry remained in her glass. She drew back the window sheer. A GTO, parked behind the battered pickup, had its lights on. Two men stood opposite one another, their bluster puncturing the night.

"Sir," odd deference in the midst of anger. "We are well within our rights to be here." This must be the missing Jay.

"My lawyer says differently and if you know what's good for ya, you'll get out. Otherwise…" The older man paused.

"Otherwise, what, sir?" Jay demanded. Grace cut across the grass to stand behind him, an indiscernible object in her hand.

"Otherwise, I, and others, will assist you in vacating my house." Patches padded the elbows of the older man's jacket, the kind duck hunters wear. The headlights illuminated mud-caked boots. No stranger to swamps this one.

Grace passed the object to Jay. The young man's face showed in the glare, draining of all restraint. Hattie flipped on her porch light, announcing her presence. She stepped outside.

"Grace, must I call the authorities to be able to get my rest?" All eyes riveted toward Hattie. She drew a steady bead on the older man's face. "Well, must I?"

The night air hung with humidity, almost too thick to breathe. A cricket's repetitive chirp stretched the moment of decision.

The older man blinked. "Sorry, ma'am." He turned back to Jay, hissing. "This isn't over." He screeched out of the driveway in a flurry of gravel and dust. Hattie shook her head. Angry men almost always sent rocks flying.

"Hattie, sorry…" Grace's sentence trailed off in the squeal of tires.

"I intend to get some sleep now and I suggest the two of you do the same." Hattie waited for them to move inside. The young man wrapped an arm around Grace, the now discernible fireplace poker extended from the other as he steered them toward their front door. Hattie turned toward hers.

"Ma'am?" Hattie swiveled her head. The young man held the door open. Grace cleared the threshold. "I just…I'm sorry we woke you."

Hattie and Jay exchanged distant looks. She nodded and stepped inside, leaving her porch light on. She peeked into Mildred's room. All was quiet.

Mildred awoke with signs of life in her left side, but it would be a slow repair. Each MS episode lessens. Dozens of attacks, each eroding muscle, undetectable until they are not, like an overnight Hollywood sensation actually years in the making. Mildred sat at the breakfast table, fielding her toast with a shaky hand, offering a review of her novel.

"While my story is quite good, I think our neighborhood drama may be better." Mildred hadn't missed the scene after all.

Hattie kept her eyes on the stove. "And I think we should mind our own business of which we have plenty."

"Since when do you want nothing of a fight?"

Hattie spooned Crisco into the cast-iron skillet and fired up the burner, rankled by Mildred's remark. She retrieved the egg carton from the fridge, welcoming the rush of cool refrigeration.

"My fight today is with our slug-infested garden, not those who blunder in the night."

Hattie cracked eggs into a mixing bowl.

"Is it now?" Mildred mocked. "I guess I'll have my eggs scrambled this morning."

"It is, and yes, you will." Hattie whipped and poured the eggs into the skillet. "And you need to mind your own business too."

Hattie had little faith that Mildred would heed her advice, having danced a lifelong jig with anti-Semitism. The sisters' social justice meters were in sync. Hattie flipped the turkey sausages in a separate pan, her kosher ways more rote than real.

Mildred sipped her coffee. "Just what do we know about her, other than her mother is dead, she's pre-law with a black boyfriend and knows how to handle a shovel?"

Such innocent inquiries from Mildred had resulted in Hattie taking on more than one case she would have otherwise left aside. For years, Mildred, a retired librarian, had served as Hattie's best sounding board, helping Hattie catalog evidence and research precedents. Those adrenalin-filled days, following the righteous path, had disappeared along with Hattie's sense of purpose. Her four-plus-decades law practice shuttered by the demands of Mildred's disease.

Hattie propelled the wooden spoon through the eggs.

"You mean other than she has a relationship that flies in the face of multiple, albeit questionable, societal norms?" Mildred did not care about such norms but Hattie knew things could get sticky.

Mildred raised her right eyebrow, as Hattie sat a full plate in front of her. "Did you catch him calling that ruffian 'sir' last night? There's more there, there." Mildred used her fork to ply the sausage apart. Today's options did not include manipulating a knife with her left hand.

"There may be, but it's not our business." Hattie busied herself with the dishes, suspecting her fine-point approach would not deter Mildred.

Mildred wheeled herself with her right hand into the door frame then around it. Hattie did not assist. Mildred needed to control of her own path as long as possible.

Hattie nestled knees-first in the dirt, surrounded by bite-pocked azalea leaves. A bucket at her side, beer in its belly, created a makeshift prison for unlucky gastropods.

Grace's rain boots edged the driveway. "You didn't tell me you were a lawyer."

Hattie's eyes moved upward. "You didn't ask." Her young neighbor's face read cloudy like the afternoon Texas sky.

"Well, people know you."

Deft at the gambit, Hattie tossed another culprit into the bucket exacting retribution. "What people?"

Grace's boots crossed the drive. "My constitutional law professor."

Malcolm taught Con Law. He had always talked too much, although she had liked to listen to him go on. Malcolm lived to test the rules. Uncertainty about her own rules creased Hattie's forehead.

"It came up that I live on Desco Drive. He said a friend of his lived on the same street." Grace punctuated her discovery with hands on her hips. "He told me your last name." Hattie would not have changed it even if she had married. But the question was withdrawn. The objection had overpowered the question.

"Did he now?" Hattie backhanded her hair off her face. The cloud filter rendered everything beautiful. The leaves marbleized. The slugs luxuriated in their beer pond.

She had said yes instead of no. A sudden stench-carrying breeze broke the beauty.

If only the neighbors would put their damn garbage can lid on tighter.

Grace pressed on. "You're Hattie Henenberg." An accusatory wrinkle in Grace's brow dared Hattie to deny. "You served on a special all-female Texas Supreme Court. You're famous." Hattie plucked off two well-chewed leaves. "And, you're a former assistant district attorney and the first female in the DA's office in Dallas, or maybe it was Texas?"

Hattie dusted the dirt off her gloves. "The key word therein is former." She sent the slugs attempting escape back into the bucket. "And, Nellie was the first." She admired the slugs' millimeter-by-millimeter persistence, their unwillingness to accept their fate mournfully familiar. "What's your point?"

"Just that it's impressive, that's all." Grace shifted in her stance. "I read up on you."

The cloud bank stretching the horizon, its length less consequential than its girth, puffed out images. Hattie's own chest in profile, a palm raised. She had softened her tailored suit with a white silk blouse and a blue satin bow the day she had been sworn in. She had been softer then.

"Well, my focus is my sister now and your focus should be your studies, not defending your boyfriend in the driveway at two o'clock in the morning."

"Jay was defending me. And, for your information, Jay works at the Legal Aid Bureau that you evidently started. My professor wouldn't shut up about you."

"Jay works at Legal Aid?" Hattie shifted to another bush.

"He volunteers when he can, second black student to graduate Mississippi Law. His job takes him out of town a lot."

"He has a job?" An old trick, goading the witness into defensive details.

Grace rose to the bait. "Yes, he does." The girl's voice held a note of defiance. "He works for Dr. King as an advance man. He goes ahead to scout the venue and—"

Hattie cut her off. "I know what advance work is." The sun teetered above the cloud, setting Hattie's perspiration factory in motion. She retrieved her handkerchief from her dungaree pocket and swiped at her forehead, eyeing the girl through its folds.

The girl took a step back. "Sorry, it's just, Jay's work is tough. The places not always welcoming." Grace ran her hands through her hair and down her face. "And now, this horrible man."

The son had inherited the house next door but the duck hunter was too old to fit that scenario. Hattie could shutter her office but not her mind. The executor of Matt Clement's estate had engaged a company to manage the property. The last occupants had moved out after Christmas, just before Grace had arrived.

Hattie pushed her handkerchief back into her pocket and fingered the small stone still resting inside. "That man. Is he the property manager?"

The girl rubbed the back of her neck. "No. I'm not a renter. I'm the owner."

The cloud bank slid apart. Hattie held her hand up to shield the glare. "Based on last night's events, I'll assume you're finding home ownership's not all it's cracked up to be?"

The girl winced. "Only when someone tries to make trouble where none should be. I inherited this house fair and square. He just doesn't want a mixed-race couple in his brother's house." Grace crossed her arms. A vein protruded from her forehead.

Mildred rolled out onto the front walk. "Hattie?" How had she manipulated the threshold with only one hand? Mildred's inner strength never failed to stun. "It's too hot to do much more. Dump those slugs and invite our new neighbor over for some lemonade."

"Well, would you like to join us?"

Grace rolled her shoulder backwards. "Lemonade sounds perfect."

The girl leaned over to offer a hand up. Annoyed more with her own lack of dexterity than the deference to age, Hattie batted it away and moved to a crouch before rising on her own.

"Give Mildred a push to the back, would you?" Hattie strode to the alleyway scrunching her nose. She dumped the beer and bodies. She secured the can's lid and that of her neighbors, snuffing out the stink. Sandstone surrounded the sisters' backyard live oak tree, providing a terraced oasis. Grace rolled Mildred next to the garden table and took the rocker.

Mildred got right to it. "Who exactly did you inherit the house from?"

Mildred could dig all she liked. Hattie had no intention of being drawn into their young neighbor's woes.

"Technically, my mother, but it was left it to my father." Grace held her glass of lemonade up to her mouth. Her eyes darted between the sisters.

Mildred spoke first. "So, your father was Matt Clement's only son, George?"

"Yes, but they had a falling out." Grace's words settled on an uncertain breeze, not flowing north or south.

Hattie filled her glass. The garden work had left her throat parched, though her armpits didn't lack for moisture. She took a seat downwind. "Where did your father and mother meet?" Hattie ignored Mildred's look of approval.

"In Atlanta, during college." Grace toes propelled the rocker back and forth. "After he died, we moved to Chicago where my godparents live."

Hattie took a long drink of lemonade. "Your father died when?"

"I was only three. We had moved to Mississippi a year or so before he...passed."

A sense of something much more surged in Hattie.

The girl leaned her head back. A squirrel leapt from one branch to another above.

Mildred patted the girl's hand. "Was there an accident?"

Grace grasped her glass. "There was...an incident. His car ran off the road." Grace took a sip of lemonade. "My godmother told me my mother felt responsible. If it wasn't for her, he might still be alive."

Unexplained deaths fascinated Hattie. "So, you believe your father was killed because of something your mother did?"

Mildred shot Hattie a smirk across the bow of the terrace.

Grace pushed out of her rocker and poured a refill. She eyed the sisters over the rim of her glass. "Not because of something she did, because of who she was." The girl hesitated, like a swimmer at the end of a high dive viewing the audience below before plunging. "My mother was mixed. Her grandfather was white, her father mostly white, her mother mixed."

Hattie folded her hands. This "mix" would make the girl, despite her skin tone to the contrary, one of only five minority women at the Methodist university, cogs in the slow-rolling wheel of integration. A sluggish creep in Texas often punctuated by violence.

Mildred's face held a multitude of concerns. "Are you saying your father was killed because he married a woman of mixed race?" The doctor's caution about Mildred becoming stressed on any level replayed inside Hattie's ear. Hattie sat her glass down with a forceful clink.

Grace flashed a look at Hattie before responding. "His car went off a cliff. If my mother knew the truth, she took it to her grave." Grace settled back into the rocker. "Anyway, her will deeded this house to me." The girl motioned next door. "I'm not sure my grandfather knew his son had died."

Mildred interjected. "If he knew, he didn't tell Harry or me." Mildred took a breath. "Matt kept his troubles to himself, especially after his wife left him. And then, his mind went."

Grace stopped rocking. "My father told my mother his parents had divorced when he was little and his mother died after that." Grace looked at Hattie. "My father died intestate. According to property law in Texas, the house should pass to my mother and then, to me."

Hattie raised an eyebrow. "Don't believe everything you read." Probate laws are not so simple when navigating multiple deaths of potential heirs. "Lots of wrenches can be thrown by angry wannabes."

"What do you mean?" Grace's face contorted.

Hattie studied the squirrel now stretched across the trunk heart. "Could be your great-uncle is basing his protest on the neighborhood covenants. Dallas remains a city of veiled segregation."

Mildred wagged her head. "They let the Jews live here now, but most realtors skirt around showing anyone other than white buyers properties in this area."

Hattie tagged on. "Despite the Supreme Court ruling against such things." She prided herself on being up-to-date on federal court cases. "Have you read the decision?" She wasn't going to do this for the girl, when the girl could help herself.

"No." Grace chewed on her lip. The squirrel retreated.

"That's what you should do next." Hattie gave her sister a pointed look. "I'm going to shower and start supper." She turned to Grace. "When I was in law school, the library wasn't open on Sundays, but I understand it is now." Hattie glanced up at the cloud blanket tucking in for the night. The storm wouldn't wait much longer.

Hattie!" Hattie threw back her covers at the whispered cry. Grace stood on her tiptoes next to her bedroom window. "Hattie, it's me."

"Grace?" Hattie, wrapped her robe around her. "Come around back." Hattie squeaked open the screen door. "It must be three a.m."

"I think someone is trying to get into my house." They backed inside. Hattie latched the door behind them. Grace shivered.

Hattie grabbed the throw off the wicker love seat and tossed it around Grace's shoulders. "Come into the front room where it's warmer."

Grace clutched the throw to her chest and followed Hattie, tracking mud on the linoleum and hardwoods as she went. "I didn't know where else to go. Jay's in Beaumont. They're on my front porch. I got out the back as fast as I could." Another shudder rocked her frame.

"You sit down." Hattie turned on her front porch light. Footsteps resounded, stamping down the sidewalk. Car headlights pierced the gloom. Engines reverberated in the night. A squeal of tires. Hattie turned back to Grace. "I think they've gone. Let me check on Mildred."

Hattie caught Mildred up on the possible intruders as they shuffled into the living room. Grace sat wide-eyed on the divan. Mildred set her cane aside and joined her.

Grace's looked up. "Should we call the police?"

"Hattie's calling the authorities now." Mildred gave Grace a squeeze.

"Yes, I'd like to report a possible crime." Hattie stretched the cord on the hall phone, taking another look out the dining room window as she spoke. "Yes, 6334 Desco Drive."

Hattie ferried the phone back to the hall stand, returning with a pair of fur-lined booties. "Take off those muddy socks." Grace slipped into the foot gear with an apologetic smile.

Mildred turned to face Grace. "What did you see before you got out?"

"Not much, just shapes. I forgot to leave the porch light on. I was in the bedroom studying. I have an exam tomorrow...uh, I guess today." Grace pulled the throw closer.

"Can you describe the men?"

"They seemed tall and they had on long coats of some kind." Grace leaned back.

Mildred reached over and took her hand. "Do you remember anything they said? The more you remember, the easier it'll be to catch the culprits." A police car pulled up.

Hattie opened the door to the two men in uniform. "Officers."

The officers surveyed the room, taking in the two seated women. "Did someone attempt a break-in here?"

"No, the scene is next door. This young lady fled out her back door when she heard possible intruders about fifteen minutes ago. They may have broken into her house."

The policemen fixed on Grace. "You heard them outside?"

Grace nodded. "I heard a clacking or clicking, too. I don't know what it was."

"OK. You three sit tight." The officers moved back into the night. Hattie padded into the kitchen. She returned with a pot of hot water, cups, saucers and a tea bag assortment on a tray.

The women sipped their tea in silence. The police returned.

The lead officer gave Hattie an odd look before addressing Grace. "We don't believe they entered your house." His words hung in the air. The clock on the mantle chimed the half hour.

The face of the younger officer read sympathetic. "But we can't be certain nothing is missing until you check."

"Do you need me to come with you now to see?"

The policemen both nodded. The young officer spoke to Hattie. "Ma'am, it might be a good idea for you to come as well."

Hattie grabbed a wrap.

Grace looked over at Mildred who held up a hand waving them off. "Don't worry about me. I'll be fine."

Hattie and Grace followed the officers down the walk. The streetlight at the corner did little to illuminate their path, its gleam stymied by the Spanish oaks bordering the sidewalk. The police had turned on Grace's porchlight. She halted midstride and sucked in her breath.

Moths buzzed the porchlight, bumping against it, not learning, attacking again, their blows muted. No clicks or clacks. The sound of the ball bouncing in spray paint could be described as a clack or a loud click when one shakes the canister.

Splayed in bright red across Grace's front door were the words: "NIGGER, GET OUT."

Grace collapsed into Hattie. They sank together onto the hard stone of the front walk.

"Tea or coffee?" Hattie stood above Grace's makeshift bed on the sewing room settee. Light streamed through the blinds. Mildred had insisted Grace stay until Jay returned from Beaumont.

Grace rubbed at the crusted sleep in the corners of her eyes. "Coffee, please. But I can make it."

Hattie gave up a rare smile. "If you think Mildred's going to let a guest get her own coffee, you've got another think coming." She motioned down the hallway. "A fresh towel is on the rack. You might use this moment to freshen up a bit." Both sisters were in the kitchen when Grace finished her shower.

"I slept later than I meant to." She twisted her damp hair at the back of her neck. "I have that exam this afternoon."

Hattie stood at the stove in an old pair of dungarees, a paint-splotched plaid shirt and well-worn shoes. A kerchief bound her hair back in a Rosie-the-Riveter imitation. "I've recorded the evidence of last night's events with my camera, as did the police. Detectives dusted for fingerprints early this morning." Grace followed Hattie's gaze. Two buckets of paint, brushes, painter's tape and a drop cloth rested in front of the sisters' back door.

"No need to let it linger," The toast popped up with a ching.

Hattie served Grace a plate.

"I have class at eleven."

Hattie took her seat. "Then we'd better get a move on." The women bent over their breakfasts.

Grace lifted her last bite to her mouth and Hattie pushed back her chair. "Time to get to it." The two women crossed their conjoined driveways and unloaded the supplies on Grace's front porch.

Hattie spoke first. "Notice, they didn't bleed onto the brick." The perpetrators had wanted to invoke fear without defacing property that might fall into white hands. Hattie pried the lid off the primer and swirled a stick in the can.

Grace stepped inside and returned in old jeans and a moth-eaten sweater, ferrying a step stool. She strung painter's tape along the doorframe while Hattie dipped her brush. Two neighbors cast furtive glances from their front yards.

"Do you think a neighbor did this?" Grace whispered.

Hattie paused in her brushstroke, the first four letters covered, only the E and R were still visible. "Maybe, but probably not. A thousand idiots live in a city this size."

The neighbors moved closer together, their heads bobbing.

Grace pressed the excess paint off her brush. "The covenants, you were right, they are in the deed." She swiped at the *E*. More neighbors strolled by, a veritable parade of interest.

Hattie stirred the stick round the bucket until the mixture became silky white again. Even white is a mix. She snorted. "It most likely doesn't say who cannot live here, only who can, right?" She did not add that in her experience, folks, intent on terrorizing, are quite controlled. "Is the deed handy?" Grace slipped back inside.

Hattie brushed across the *G-F-T*. The collie owners passed by shaking their heads.

Grace reemerged, tracing her finger down the page "Here it is, the third paragraph." Hattie traded her brush for the documents. Grace attacked the *O*.

Hattie read out loud. "Said property shall be used by white persons except these covenants shall not prevent occupancy by domestic servants of different race or nationality in the employ of the tenant." Hattie scanned the document from top to bottom and then flipped to the previous page. "This covenant was written in 1956, eight years after the U.S. Supreme Court ruled such things illegal."

Hattie set the papers down on the porch bench with a rue smile. "Never underestimate the guile of old white men. I assume you're not interested in being your great-uncle's maid?" Grace's laugh ignited an odd surge of relief inside Hattie.

The girl painted over the *U* with three steady strokes. "No, my career aims are a bit loftier." Hattie observed the girl's strong smooth strokes, the determination on her face. The look of a lawyer Malcolm used to say. Grace turned to Hattie. "Seriously, a judge can't uphold the covenant with the Supreme Court ruling in place, could they?"

Hattie delivered her bad news with a wry smile. "As your Con Law professor might say, the proclivity for misinterpreting the law is rampant in the Jim Crow south." Hattie painted from the opposite side covering the *T* as she spoke. "Early in the century, one of my colleagues, Edith Wilmans, divorced her husband. Back then, property rights for women were still being established but there were plenty of precedents to support her case. Despite Hortense and my efforts, the judge let her ex abscond with many of her mother's prized possessions anyway." Hattie finished painting the bottom of the door and began lightly stroking the frame where a few red streaks strayed. "Some things have changed, others haven't."

Grace stopped painting and looked at Hattie. "Hortense Ward? From the special court? She led the campaign that gave women the vote in this state, right?"

"Yes. Spent her career fighting for women's property rights." Hattie finished off the doorframe. Every door needed a solid frame. "She married a good guy the next time around."

Hattie motioned to Grace. "The *R* is all yours."

Grace dipped her brush back in the bucket. The gossipy neighbors melted away. With strong, assured strokes, Grace brushed away the *R*.

The funny thing about last straws is they surprise you. The others having been plucked away with little recognition.

Hattie slid her hand into her pocket and fingered the stone, one Malcolm could skip five times across the water. He would be amused to find her involved. Again.

"Your primer's complete." She laid her brush down, making a mental list of next steps. A frame she could provide. Sureness came from within. "Up to you to apply the next coat."

The girl needed to believe she could do it herself.

The Body under Late-Stage Capitalism

Karin Spitfire

This poem first appeared in Issue 95 of Burningword Literary Journal

The heart has abdicated feeling.
I have enough to do, all this beating, all this pumping.
Builds a wall to harden the pericardium.
Feels the shearing less.
Knows it is ultimately useless and easily scaled,
the breakthrough scorching.

In the heart's determined absence,
the digestive track takes up the slack, but can't stomach it.
Bile, bubbling lava, ire, rise along the esophageal membranes.
What does make it down is hardly digestible,
only present due to the sheer volume of forced feeding.
The small intestine is especially overworked,
separating the pure from the *unpure*, the true from the untrue,
the useful from the corrupted, too big a job.
so nearly all passes on to the large intestine,
which just wants more water.

The lungs, the lungs are crying,
damp or charred,
ash floating, hacking up bits of themselves,
too many fires burning, too many on the edge of the last exhale.
Seeking solace on hard granite,
weep into the mother's embrace
even as she suffers.

The nervous system is trigger-happy.
The hand tremors unrelenting.
Good time not to have a gun.

The interstitial swamps,
lowdown fluids between/among
everything,
are in the best shape, not frozen, not making off
with the last energy in the treasury.
Steady, slow, tidal,
still taking cues from the moon

but in need of water.

The feet run.
The hands want to strangle.
The spine contorts under jeopardy.
The endocrine system would just like
the right drugs to fuck its brains out.

The mouth and vocal chords,
more inarticulate than not,
garble, gurgle, sputter, spewing
silent.

The central canal, the core,
aligning with the earth's magma
roaring, roiling
unconcerned with blue, waits
for vents, fissures, some pore, some open vein
to come erupting out
with precision and deadly aim.

But the cells
in their unwavering, egalitarian democracy,
in their trillions, all still work together,
each with its small input, need, job,
praying
in this way to keep the whole alive.

The mind, once tethered by the heart, is disembodied,
wracked in this climate of isolation.
shouting for water. ⬤

Eulogy for My Mother

She wore a vast variety of blue headgear year round
some of the time she wore lots of green
at the nursing home they would laugh
'cause for no discernable reason
the variegated greens had to be worn on top
but then would change
to having to be her bottoms
about this she was quite adamant
as if her life depended on it
with the green there were also snowy white bottoms
which sometimes proved problematic
but she insisted.

Everything around her was a cacophony of colors and shapes
polka dots, florals
her walls, dahlias, chrysanthemums
she stipulated a jaguar hidden in the leaves, wild monkeys
and palm fronds toward the south
sunrise and sunset, of course facing the east and west
the east with the ocean and its critters
west with mountains, puma and grizzly
she did let the north be just blue and white
and underfoot-well every new CNA was either
freaked out or oblivious to the riot to creepy crawlers
and yes, above half was blue with white clouds
and the other the night sky
there were endless discussions before
she decided what phase of the moon and the time of year
the stars would shine.

The staff and patients would find
all sorts of reasons and excuses to visit her because
being next to her was like going outside
when you came to see her she would always ask you to sing
if you would do a jig, tap, or recite poetry even better
and she'd ask you how you were and after your children and your children's children.

Being the force of nature
she was able to convince the CNAs

to get her in the wheelchair van and
drive her to not one but two of those few accessible nature parks
when she got there she had long serious talks
with the lichen and moss, and granite
then giggles and quips with the swamp grasses, boggy peat, intertidal mud.

As time passed she left her sanctuary less and less
sometimes she'd force the nurses to take her
to watch the news, nothing else
then she would weep for days

When the power grid went down,
which it did more and more,
She'd have them push her and anyone else who would come
into the dark to stare at the Milky Way.

When she did leave her room
the other residence would stir, stare,
become weepy, glad, something
The collective energy of the place notched up
My mother's presence did that
And when she smiled sometimes there would be mayhem.

In the end,
well, it is too gruesome to talk about
besides none of us were around
she was left to her own devices
to heal her scorched skin,
fracking, wounds, poisoned blood stream
to metabolize all the carnage
and remember her beauty. ⓜ

Residue

Essential tremor is commonly described as an action tremor

I shake
my left hand mostly,
it makes some people nervous,
sometime I am nervous
sometimes I'm not,
sometimes my whole body shakes

There is not one myth in the western world of daughter killing father.

These nerves to the left hand,
This group of muscles
can't completely resolve
the simultaneous impulses
to never reach out to him again
or cut his jugular

now he's dead of his own accord

I shake
the death rattle
and sing freedom ⊕

Pronouns

Deborah Schmedemann

Pronouns: Written January 2017; Revised June 2020

This particular day, January 20, 2017, I am glad to have people to see, a place to go, a task to do.

At 7:30 a.m., a motley assemblage of Chicago commuters and I board the el together at the Rockwell Station, claim our seats and settle in, cast our eyes away from each other. Two stops later, I disembark, work my way down the stairs and out the station against the crowd. I dodge the commuters streaming toward me as I head north to my daughter Mary's apartment and think: what a blessing to retire young so that I can care for my grandson today.

A block before Mary's street, I cross over to the drugstore to—do I really want to do this?—buy the morning newspapers.

At Mary's apartment, I receive my briefing: Luke will nap around noon, a furniture delivery is expected sometime during the day, she will come home late in the afternoon. Mary's employer, a non-profit working against racial and economic injustice in Illinois, gave its employees the day off, but she decided to work anyway.

Not too long after Mary leaves, eighteen-month-old Luke awakes. We sink into the couch to read. We zip through an alphabet book, read about a cheery blue truck and a mean brown truck, and linger on a story of a boy who treasures a snowy day. "I see 'now!" There is no snow today; it is a mild mid-winter day.

Energized now, Luke toddles laps around the living room and dining bay, as he gathers his fleet of vehicles: a big bus, a dump truck, an airplane. He pushes them around the room, randomly, it seems. He disappears down the hall and returns with a wad of toilet paper, which he shreds into balls and loads onto the bus.

The first eleven: George, John, Thomas, James, James, John, Andrew, Martin, William, yet another John, and yet another James.

I head for the kitchen to make Luke's snack. He scampers behind me: "'Nack? 'Nack?" He stops at his miniature kitchen, where he whisks imaginary soup in a pot. I set a plate with blueberries, apple slices, and his favorite crackers beside him. He munches, whisks, munches, whisks.

After snack, we bundle up lightly for outdoor time. We must be nearby in case the delivery service comes, so we stay on his block. On our first lap, he toddles, staring at his feet and the pavement; he veers to his right to look into a tiny side yard; he wanders into the grassy, muddy space between the sidewalk and the street. On our second lap, he kicks at the rocks lining the side yard, he picks up a few mucky sticks, and he hugs the big tree opposite his door. As I peel Luke from the tree, I feel a chill in his fingers, and we head inside.

The second eleven: Zachary, Millard, Franklin, James, Abraham (I have been told I am distantly related to him on my mother's side), Andrew, Ulysses, Rutherford, James (goodness—a lot of those!), Chester, Grover.

Mary has left us a hearty mix of macaroni and cheese with vegetables for lunch; I make an English muffin with lemon hummus for myself too. As we sit side by side, Luke pulls out most of the vegetables, deposits some on the table and drops others on the floor, then eats the macaroni and a few incidental carrots and peas. When he spies me eating my muffin, his eyes light up. He taps his fingers together in the American Sign Language symbol for *more* and calls out "more!" Of course, I give him half of my muffin.

It is nearly noon, Luke's nap-time. This morning, Mary told me of his new routine: no more bottle, no more sleep-sack to zip him into, no more reading. We head into his room for a diaper change and . . . what? I sit with him

Edrece Stansberry

in my lap, in his rocker, in his still dark room. I tell him what a lucky boy he is, to be healthy and safe, to have such wonderful parents, to be loved by so many people. He leans into my shoulder, sucking one thumb, pulling at his earlobe with the other hand, lightly tapping my calf with his feet.

As Luke naps, I sit in the stillness of the apartment's dining bay, drink green tea, and read parts of the newspaper. During my other granny-nanny shifts, I have worked on my writing during Luke's naps. But this morning, I decided: I am just too defeated to think today. So I left my writing projects at home. I set aside the news sections of the papers and delve into the minutiae of the sports pages and the drivel of the entertainment section. I work all of the puzzles.

The third eleven: Benjamin, Grover, William, Theodore, William, Woodrow, Warren (quite a few W-names those decades), Calvin, Herbert, Franklin, Harry.

After an hour and a half, Luke cries to let me know he is awake. Once his wailing plays out, we move into our spiral of afternoon play. I stack his pastel half-balls from largest to smallest; Luke knocks them down. "Oh, no!" Luke stacks five letter blocks and knocks them over. "Oh, no!" Soon vehicles from his fleet traverse our floor play. Mid-play, Luke springs up and calls out, "'RUCK!" I listen closely: yes, indeed, a truck is running outside. We move to the dining bay windows, where I set Luke standing in front of me on a chair to watch the activity.

A big, bright orange city truck is pulling a trailer on which sits a heavy-duty road-grading machine. The driver is having trouble turning from the alley into the street. A co-worker sits in the cab of the truck; three others stand here and there yelling instructions, encouragement, or (I suspect) choice words at the driver. After about ten minutes, the tricky maneuver is accomplished, and the three outsiders climb into the cab. The crew hangs out for a bit longer, jabbering, checking their cell-phones, perhaps awaiting instructions—and also, of course, blocking the street.

Luke is mesmerized by this routine city skit. As the driver finally revs the engine to roll on out, he happens to look up at our window and spots Luke. He waves at the toddler in the first floor window, who waves back at him. Luke yells, "Bye, big 'ruck!" as the truck lumbers down the street. I can almost hear Luke sigh from the thrill of it all.

My lifetime's eleven: Dwight, John (Jack), Lyndon, Richard, Gerald, James (Jimmy), Ronald, George (the dad), William (Bill), George (the son), Barack.

I doubt that "truck" was one of my first words. No, as a little girl, I was obsessed with stuffed animals and dolls. I recall that these imaginary friends overran my bed and every corner of my room by the time I was in grade school in the 1960s. By then, I lived a stone's throw from Washington, D.C., the site of so many memorials to our nation's history.

On school field trips and with my family, I often visited the Smithsonian's National Museum of American History. No exhibit called to me, the daughter of a skilled seamstress, like the collection of the First Ladies' dresses, that winding dark exhibit hall with the spot-lit displays. The lifeless mannequins garbed in elegant gowns were both macabre and glamorous. I would wander through the centuries and wonder what it would be like to wear such weird dresses (what was under those bustles?). Nobody I knew wore poufy pink skirts with embedded rhinestones like Mamie Eisenhower's, or ivory silk sheaths like Jackie Kennedy's, or brilliant yellow tent-coats with fur at the sleeves like Lady Bird Johnson's. I did not fully understand why these women were called "First Ladies" (who were the second and third?). Yet I understood from their regalia that they were important, somehow, to our country. Of course, I realized that they were all women.

I was less entranced during my childhood visits to the trinity of presidential monuments. The Washington Monument was a very tall, oddly shaped building that was fun to go up in and look down from, but that was about it. The Thomas Jefferson and Lincoln Memorials were imposing stone caverns with huge sculptures of old men. Until I could appreciate their words as clarion calls in tempestuous times, I sensed only that these men must have been very important. Of course, I realized that Washington, Jefferson, and Lincoln were all men.

No doubt, every textbook I read as a child referred to a president of the United States with male pronouns. Why would I question this? A stone's throw from my school were the First Ladies' dresses (so graceful, so pretty) and the male presidents' monuments (so marble, so massive).

Yet, somehow, I did not internalize a lesson about myself in any of this. By mid-elementary school, I had two equally firm life goals: to write children's books or to be a diplomat/spy. My second career path was inspired by the fathers in my neighborhood. (Yes, a CIA agent lived across the street from my family.) Why did I not hew more to the paths of the home-maker mothers around me?

I attribute my thinking to my parents' attitude towards me from birth: My father was the only son of his father. My older sister and I were born fairly late to our parents, so I was understood to be the last of my father's line. Some in my father's family hoped that I would be a boy to carry on their unusual last name, so I suppose I disappointed them. However, my parents made it clear that they were just fine with my gender, and I should be too. I took from their attitude that I controlled my life choices.

Over my adult decades, I have taught thousands of female—and male—law students of various ages. I have represented women in poverty (some of them subject to domestic abuse). I have sheltered and counseled teenage girls in foster care. I have come to realize that my experience as a female is far from universal; so too my mindset. I now realize that hundreds of years of First Ladies' dresses and hundreds of tons of marble memorializing only male presidents can make for a skewed view of life's possibilities. Reading only "he"/"him"/"his" in sentences about presidents can etch expectations into a person's psyche.

Around 5:00, Mary comes home. The delivery driver shows up then too—another 'ruck—with a rolled-up mattress he somehow thrusts into the apartment all by himself. Mary and I bundle Luke up, secure him in his stroller, and head out to pick up a light dinner. Now dusk, light is giving way to dark, a reflection of our moods this entire day.

A few blocks into our walk, my fists wedged deep into my coat pockets, I ask Mary, "Did you listen to the speech?"

She responds, "I couldn't watch. But I thought I should listen. It seemed short."

"I couldn't even listen."

Back in her apartment as we munch our lukewarm pizza, we talk about what to write on our poster for the Chicago Women's March the next day. My other daughter will be joining us. I tell Mary that protest marches are more her thing than mine; I will be fine with whatever she comes up with. But she and I both know that I came of age during the Civil Rights era, I have written volumes as a law professor, and I am rarely at a loss for words. It is just that on this day, in particular, I am too defeated to think.

Had my wish been granted, on this January 20, Mary, Luke, and I would have gathered in front of a TV. We would have dressed Luke in red, white, and blue and positioned him on the couch between us. We would have plied him with his favorite snacks to keep him awake and stacked his favorite books in his lap to keep him from wandering off. We would have clapped and cheered, and he would have, too, in time with us.

Luke would have been mesmerized by the spectacle unfolding on the screen; it would have been his first time watching TV. Mary and I would have been mesmerized, too. For Mary, it would have been the passing of power from a president she revered to a president she would hope to come to respect. For me, it would have been the realization of a dream that my country would someday elect a woman to its highest office.

Hillary—the first female. Not.

Some future January, Luke and I will make our way to Washington, D.C. He may be five then, or perhaps nine.

Crap; this needs editing. Scratch five. Not Kamala; out on December 3. Not Amy; out on March 3. Not Elizabeth; out on March 5. Not Tulsi; out on March 20. *Joe, please let it be Joe.* I will keep nine. Dare I write only nine? Am I that sure? Should I hedge my bets: nine or thirteen? How old will **I** be when this finally happens?

Mary will go with us for sure; perhaps other relatives will join our pilgrimage. We will take the train, so Luke can see some of the glamorous and gritty cities, sprawling suburbs, pretty hamlets and dying little towns, wintering prairies, and rugged mountains that constitute these United States.

I will show Luke the memorials to his nation's presidential history. We will wander through the centuries among the First Ladies' dresses and marvel at the monuments. We will make a special visit to the National Portrait Gallery to gaze at the portrait of President Obama: dressed in a black suit and open white shirt, sitting amid a vibrant bower with flowers symbolizing his roots in Kenya, Hawaii, and Chicago. I will tell Luke that my father Keith adored this president, his last one; that there should be a Kansas sunflower in the painting because this president's mother was a Kansan, as was Keith; and that this president made many people feel, for the first time, that they could be president one day.

Then we will take our places on the National Mall, that grand expanse holding the public waiting to glimpse, to hear, to cheer on the new president. I will buy Luke a big bag of souvenirs, and we will take slews of selfies. We will stand with the million-plus enthralled people who are actually there to celebrate the new era. No matter Luke's age, I will hold his hand and squeeze it when she starts to speak.

Luke may wonder why it matters that the new president is a woman. Mary will tell her son that it is time for the country to be led by a woman because women may lead differently than men. I will tell Luke that it matters to me for one decades-old reason and one much newer reason. Raising two daughters, I wanted them to believe that they could grow up to be whatever they wanted to be—including president of their country. And as a grandmother of a boy, I want my grandson to believe that girls can grow up to be whatever they want to be—including president of his country.

Late January 20, 2017: Just before Luke goes to bed, he helps his mother make a sign for his mother, his grandmother, and his aunt to carry at the Chicago Women's March. He sits on the poster-board on which Mary writes in bold black letters: NO HUMAN BEING IS ILLEGAL. Luke scribbles on the poster with red and purple crayons.

When Mary returns from the march, she will place this sign in one of the windows in their dining bay, where Luke will stand beside it as he takes in the outside world for years to come.[1]

1   This essay is dedicated to Luke, whose own first protest sign (written when he was four) reads, "No one is better than each other."

Forced Feedings

Abby Brunt

*("A suffragette being force-fed with a nasal tube" from
The Suffragette by Sylvia Pankhurst, 1911)*

Writing a paper for a college class,
I find her: the suffragette force-fed,
photo after photo. In this one
Emily Davison is lying prone, face
hazy with ether, eyes rolled back
into her head. The camera captures
her shame. She is unable to resist.
Her hand holds the armrest of the chair,
the doctor's assistant pins her down,
grips her thigh. The doctor
has inserted a long tube through her nose
into her stomach. Two women squeeze
pulped food from a bulb.

Seeing it, I feel a gnawing pain,
not unlike hunger, in the pit
of my own belly. A memory emerges
like an old yellowed photo: I am eight,
huddled in the corner of a room, shrinking
as if I could hide behind the walls.
I hear whining high and thin
winding along the inside of my skull.

I watch my mother straddle
a small boy she babysat, watch her
pinch his nose shut, shove food
into his gasping mouth. His arms
flail helplessly as he chokes and cries.
She is a fortress, stone-faced, she won't
be moved. She pushes each bite
through his lips, holds his nose
until he swallows—she doesn't let up.
His cries become hiccups, silence follows.
No more tears or struggle, he opens

his mouth on cue, arms limp at his side.

Tears fill my eyes, I refocus
on the suffragette. I wonder what
is resistance made of and when
do we break? In the photo,
Emily seems to have given in—
force throttling her spirit.
Later, released from prison,
she threw herself in front of the king's
horse, and he trampled her to death. ⓡ

Self Portrait: Daughter

Here, I know my place, know
how these four walls lead
to other walls—spaces
I fill with domestic tasks.
Small children cry in the church
nursery, nudging my breast.
A two-month-old wants milk
and her three-year-old brother
looks at me in scorn, wants to know
why won't I feed her? I tell him
I can't. He scoffs, deciding I'm useless.
I feel Eve's curse squeeze
my insides, her blood
running out, soaking the pad
in my underwear. I am careful
to sit upright so as not to make
a mess of it: my womanhood.
I don't want it pooling here
on the church floor. I'm told
there's nothing left to do
but locate the steeple, erect
and pointing its way toward God.
But I'm not waiting for my future
to be spearheaded. I've got
another point in mind.
With my ballpoint pen, I write
letters from Patriarchy's outpost,
leaving myself a trail of words,
names to trace my way out:
Susan B. Anthony, Elizabeth Cady Stanton,
Harriet Tubman, Gloria Steinem,
Coretta Scott King, Madeleine Albright.
On the network news
I hear Hillary Clinton proclaim
Women's rights are human rights.
It feels like she's talking to me. ❦

Womenspeaking #1

Nodding ~~our heads~~ often
    ~~to show~~ we are listening
          to the sermon. The hymnals open
    ~~we sing~~ only sweetly.
        Honey~~ed phrases~~ repeating
        ~~as credo~~
    dripping from pink lips.
    We comb through ~~pages~~
        never ~~questioning~~
          do ~~we~~
          ~~believe?~~

The ~~great~~ man lectures
    ~~at the front of the room~~. We sit
        ~~there~~ in our ~~place, aware of the growing~~
    silence like bees
        ~~in our brains~~, the ~~nauseous~~
          buzzing
~~louder~~ with each burne~~d word~~
~~we hear~~, falling
        like ash from his lips.
~~It~~ only ~~makes sense—~~
    he is
    ~~on fire.~~

This ~~passion~~ must be his
    ~~pleasure~~, endless ~~desire—the sam~~e desire
        ~~we feel~~, coating
    ~~our bodies,~~
        ~~whetting~~
          the appetite,
but the only wetness ~~comes~~
    from our eyes,
        put~~ting~~ out
        ~~the fire~~.

~~We wonder,~~
    is there any hope

for us to be ~~satisfied?~~
~~The crawling gnaw,~~
          ~~opening in our bellies, yearning~~
                    ~~for~~ more.

Or do we simply
          end
          ~~with hunger?~~ 🌑

Ehimetalor Akhere Unuab

Shift

Susan Caggiano

My parents paneled the living room of our house in a dark, grooved, fake woodgrain that reminded me of a cave or a hollow in a tree that smelled of stale *El Producto* blunts and warm Budweiser, Tareyton 100s and rosé wine. I used to hide there, pressed against the coolness, tracing my fingers along the grooves, and following them panel by panel, as high as I could reach - imagining they formed a map that might lead me somewhere. No matter how many times I followed those lines, they only led me to the front door we never used.

Our house in Concord was nearly identical to every other house on the street – a phenomenon that only occurred on our side of town. When I was young, I learned from a friend who lived on the *right* side of the highway that my neighborhood was built for Italian and Irish immigrant mill workers. My parents bought the house from Patricio "Patsy" Ianiello, an ancient crank who yelled at us every time we went into his garden. We were a family of six and lived in a rented duplex behind his house. Just before I turned seven years old, I learned that he had offered to sell his house "cheap" so my father could buy it. I was surprised at his generosity, and after I mused aloud about his tendency to shout at us, heavily accented with an ever-angry face, Dad responded with, "Well, he's Italian."

We moved into the house during the weekend of my 7th birthday in January 1973. The house had two bedrooms upstairs and one walk-in pantry that the small army of my carpenter uncles quickly converted to a bedroom for my big brother, Sean. They also installed a doorframe in another small room that had a wide opening from the kitchen – perhaps an effort at a dining room – to make a bedroom for Sheila, my older sister. My younger sister, Jan, and I were installed in bunk beds in the tiny upstairs bedroom near my parents' room. Later, they paneled the cramped living room, and when all of us were in there at the same time, a rarity reserved for Special Occasions, Jan and I had to sit on the floor. But it was all ours, and we felt rich.

That feeling lasted only until my best friend in sixth grade invited me to sleep at her house on the other side of town. Her bedroom was the size of my family's living room and her siblings all had rooms like that. She and her sister had their own bathroom, shared by way of sliding pocket doors on both sides. Her mother drove a new expensive car. Their yard, tended by an old Italian guy I sometimes saw on my side of town, looked like a public park with its perfect arrangement of maple trees, green expanses of cool-under-your-feet grass, and beautiful hydrangeas bursting blue and purple-blossomed puffs in the spring.

One winter Sunday, when I was 9 or 10, the rain drove against my bedroom window in icy sheets, which by nightfall would turn to sleet and snow. The house was uncharacteristically quiet for a Sunday afternoon - but it was also winter, which meant Dad was home and between sports seasons – he hated basketball. "Football, baseball, and golf were the only respectable sports," he once said to me while explaining why the Red Sox manager went to the mound, "Slow, methodical thinking is what's required, there," he said, shaking his beer at me, "none of that shifty, fast-moving, jumping around. Strategy. Strategy is the thinking man's game." Then he spilled his beer on me, the chair and himself, jumping up in a rage swearing out loud. The thinking man. While he ranted, I ran to get a rag – my inner voice shouting – *fix it, fix it, NOW!*

Stillness in the house was always a hard read. It was a risk to go downstairs, to see what an idle and silent Dad might bring. But I was hungry. And bored. I moved away from the rain's comforting rhythm and headed to the kitchen. I approached the kitchen quietly, but not too quietly. He was making a sandwich. His hands were a bellwether. Steady and precise meant it might be a good day. But shaky, or worse - jerking or slamming - and trouble was brewing. I relaxed against the counter as he carefully laid each slice of the bologna on the bread, mustard neatly slathered.

"Want one?" He asked.

"Yeah. Where's Mum?"

"The club."

"A double?" I asked.

"Yeah," he said, handing me the sandwich he'd just made for himself, without looking up at me. "The club" was our ironic euphemism for her grueling work as a waitress at Nashawtuc Country Club, an exclusive club whose membership fees, likely more than my parents' annual wages, were paid so they could go to "the club" and be served.

Whenever the phrase "a double" is mentioned, it holds the power to unnerve me still. Double shifts poked life-sized holes into the fabric of our family. As a young girl, 7, or 10, or even 12, I did not understand the compulsion my mother felt to "do a double" – she never said no. I had no idea what saying "yes" to doubles meant to our family's security. I learned much later, maybe even after my own motherhood had begun, that doing doubles protected whatever earned material and social capital we had – we lived on a sharp edge that relentlessly knicked and scraped the flesh of our family's survival.

When I first learned the word *thrive*, I slipped it into my lexicon under the category of words-to-use-when-telling-stories. My teacher, who used it in a motivational lecture to my sixth or seventh-grade class – a time just before my long relationship with truancy would begin – said that the goals of education were to help us thrive. Since none in my family was a model of thriving, this inspirational speech only delivered tight knots of shame. Thriving was as alien a concept as quantum physics might be; we existed in a kind of familial dark age that seemed an inescapable part of God's Grand Plan, centuries-old, ordained, and immutable. I knew that I was expected to thrive – teachers told me that was my purpose. To me, the idea was preposterous, and if they were oh-so-wrong about this, they might be wrong about *everything* and should not be trusted.

But if the idea of thriving was understood at any level in my family, it was strictly something other people, rich people, enjoyed – Kennedy and Rockefeller rich, Boston Brahmin rich, country club rich. We understood thriving only abstractly, as something other families might do or have because of luck, or God's *grace*, a grace which rarely touched my family, and caused me to wonder what we,

or I, had done to be so without it. And that question as I grew older condensed into a coiled spring of anger and destruction that would define my choices for years to come.

Almost no one I knew had parents who worked double shifts, even on my side of town. I had one friend whose father was a firefighter and often lived at the station, sometimes for days at a time – she was clearly proud of her father and cheerfully endured his absences. My mother waitressed at the country club where my school friends went to swim at the Olympic-sized pool, play golf and eat dinner on Sundays, and Thanksgiving, and Christmas *et cetera* with their thriving families. My father sold vacuum cleaners and sewing machines at Sears, but at least he wore a suit to work.

When Mum worked a double, she would leave late morning and often not return until after I went to sleep. I developed the habit of asking what her schedule was so I could prepare myself for it. Her double shifts were also mine. By nine, or ten, as the eldest remaining daughter in the house, though only by eighteen months, I became responsible for my younger sister, Jan. My parents tasked me with chores and small cooking – by eight-years-old, I had already become adept at a dinner of grilled cheese and canned tomato soup. On days when Dad had to close, having worked his own double at Sears, Mum came home between shifts to prepare dinner and leave again, and Dad would return home just before bedtime. Those were bad days when both parents were absent. But Sundays, and other holidays, were worse when he was home, and she wasn't.

Massachusetts had blue laws restricting both retail and alcohol sales on Sundays and holidays, so as a retail salesman, my father was home on Sundays, unlike Mum. She usually had to work Sundays. That was an important day at Nashawtuc – whole families would come for their after-church Sunday meal. Mum would sometimes get up early to go to church and then go to work, but when our parish offered Saturday evening Mass, she'd go then, unless she worked a double. So, on Sundays, Dad would be "it," and it was always fraught.

The blue laws meant a parent would be home, but that mercurial parent directed our family's turbulent weather like a small god, drunk or not. I once entered an adult discussion of these laws with an almost desperate agreement, "They are so stupid!" They laughed at my fervor not seeing that I had my own reasoning. I wanted the drinking adults – father, uncles, and even my brother, to go to work and leave me and my sisters in solitude. They wanted to buy a case of Schlitz and Seagram's Seven whiskey. If our father had not gone to the liquor store on Saturdays, the weather in the house broiled. If he had gone, the cloying smell of stale beer or whiskey and cheap cigars created waves of fear and anxiety; it was a child's guess at the weather to come. There was no winning for us on Sundays.

That one Sunday was less fraught than most because I was alone with him. Most times that worked out because when only the two of us were home he could ratchet it down a bit. His demeanor in the quiet of the house became less authoritarian, and more *Daddy*. So, when *Daddy* was around, it felt joyous. Yet, it wasn't really joy, as I learned decades later. It was simply the absence of pain, the absence of fear, and unaffected relief at the absence of shame.

On that day, while we silently ate lunch together, we decided to play Scrabble. I like to remember that he offered to play the game with me, but it easily (and more likely) could have been me who had asked. We were alone, and I was in the fourth grade. I had just that year been moved to the fifth-grade language arts class in my split-grade classroom, where fourth and fifth-grade students mingled according to skill level. In spelling and reading, I was ahead of my peers and placed with the older students for learning. I always placed in the top three in our weekly spelling bee - and even 5th graders wanted me on their team. So, I thought Scrabble could be my game.

The game began with some competitive teasing. He reminded me of the loss I took in miniature golf the previous summer. I reminded him of his because Jan had won that match. But this banter was deeply unfamiliar to my father, his attempts to joke or be playful were awkward and forced. Even as a child, I knew it wasn't quite right – it felt both desperate and precious – and filled me with a compulsive desire to please, which was tempered only by a deepening sense of dread.

We set the game up on a small table next to the only bookshelf in the house, a tall, narrow shelf. On it were Dad's favorite books: Mathew Brady's photo documen-taries of the Wild West and the Civil War, and the family Bible with our names listed, absent those of my older brother and sister's. When I asked my mother about their omitted names, she said, "They have a different Dad." End. Of. Discussion. I knew they had different last names, but I thought nothing of it – they were my family. Another time, I learned from gossip at Nana's house that I had another brother, killed before I was born by the driver of a tractor-trailer who could not stop for the two-year-old dashing into the street. I called my cousin a liar and punched her arm - hard - for telling me such a terrible thing. Of course I would know about a dead brother. I spent the rest of the day facing a corner in Nana's kitchen for that outburst. When I returned home, my mother said nothing but led me to the bureau in her room, always off-limits to my siblings and me. She opened a drawer full of lacy things, and drew out a photograph of a cherubic boy, smiling at me from the past. "His name was Kevin. He is with God now." And she left me in the room with his photo in my small hand.

Next to the family Bible sat one of my favorite books – a worn-out, blue fabric-covered *Noah Webster's Dictionary* – my secret weapon – and it gave me great power in my family. The more words I could have, the more power I would have. If I used a "smart" word, heaps of praise came from all quarters. "Look at her, one day she'll be a lawyer!" "Look at how smart she is, Jack, you've got trouble on your hands." To his credit, Dad would often scoff at that, saying there was nothing wrong with having a smart girl – one of the gifts he left in his tumultuous wake.

This dictionary, with little blue threads hanging from the corners, was *my* Bible. Despite the worn and faded fabric, the cover was velvety and rich, and I often sat in a corner, hidden away on the floor, or sometimes in a closet with a flashlight, using the powers of osmosis to make sense of the world and consolidate my power. I stroked the corners where the fabric was worn down to the pulpy layers of cardboard that were separating and fanning out so that I could strum the layers as I tried to sound out and memorize words I had heard. Pugnacious – a teacher had called me that once. Episcopal was written on the church my mother told me to avoid, "That's a Protestant church," she whispered in the voice parents use to warn children of dangerous things, "don't go there – we're Catholic."

Irrepressible – my Uncle Andy had once called me, and when I read it, I felt a surge of pride straighten my back; I also looked up imp as he said that too – as in irrepressible imp – and that surge of pride became a powerful elixir that thrilled me. Words had become my scripture.

After setting up the tiles for Scrabble, I placed the word, *herb*, at the juncture of the word *house* that he'd just laid down, and with the condescending tone that I would learn soon enough was not just the tone of a stern father, but of many men I would come to know, he challenged the word.

"*Herb*, has no, *h*, Suzy. It starts with *E. E-R-B. Erb.*" Then he added in consolation a nod to the fact that I was a fourth-grader, "But, I'll let you try again. Go on."

I was full of my earned power. This. This was it. I knew something he did not – it was my moment to shine and make him proud.

"Dad, I *know herb* has an *h*, I learned in school. It's a silent *h*, but it *IS* spelled that way!" My tone was meant to be adult-like, smart sounding. But in my first attempt at this tone, I sounded petulant and almost as condescending as him.

He scoffed, affronted. His shoulders raised, and he put both hands on his knees – a warning signal – and the small god spoke louder, pointed his finger at the board, "Silent *h*, eh? I don't believe you. Erb. E-R-B." His back straightened. His lips narrowed. Impulsively, I ignored these early signs of impending weather. I insisted that it was spelled *h-e-r-b*. He did not withdraw the challenge. Exasperated, I reached out for *my* bible, Webster's *Book of Power*, and

proceeded to show him that *herb* was definitively spelled *h-e-r-b*.

"See right there. *That* is how you spell *herb*, Daddy." What came next should have been a moment that in a healthy relationship would have passed in humor – a silly moment when the cards were flipped, and the Dad learns from his daughter. But in that moment, the weather changed, darkened, and the room shrank to the small space around our Scrabble game.

"Look at that," he said a little too softly, his eyes retreating, "I always spelled it without the h – maybe that's how I was taught." His voice seemed very far away too, as if all of him, his *Daddiness*, his solidity, simply evaporated in a breath. What was left behind was not a real person, not even a small god – just a slip of bones and a dead whisper.

"Ah, here. I've got a word for you!" He rushed to place new tiles down.

I hardly remember the rest of the game. His brow deepened, his movements became more furtive and impatient. If I took too long to make a new word, he fidgeted and taunted me to come up with one. I stopped trying to win and just put down whatever word could get us to the end of the game. Daddy had left the room, replaced by little demons who affirmed his deep belief that he was as stupid as he thought and that his daughter, in shame, would turn away from him. But in that moment, I knew little of those demons of his, though I would reckon with each of them as I grew older. What I did know was that I had the power to diminish my father, to erase a small god. It was terrifying. ⊕

Voiceover

Jillian Danback-McGhan

When the episode aired on its designated evening, Ellie realized the producers had changed her voice.

Confined with the television screen's shiny black border, she watched her own figure, standing in front of the grey warship behind her, clad in her dark blue uniform overalls emblazoned with the gold stitching and insignia designating her as the ship's Commanding Officer.

Her ship. Her face. Her name at the bottom of the screen.

Not her voice.

"There must be some mistake," Ellie said, gaping at the screen long after her feature ended. Incensed, and a little embarrassed by comments from the few friends who joined her at her home to watch the episode ("Nice voice, sir!"; "Is your name Ellie Apple or Adam's Apple???"), she stopped by the Public Affairs Office the next morning to ascertain the cause of this bizarre decision.

"There was no mistake," Captain Thaddeus Guy, the Public Affairs Officer, informed her.

"Could you tell me why my voice was lowered a few octaves, then?" She asked, glaring at Captain Guy intensely.

She recorded the segment over 3 months ago for *Weekly World,* a popular Sunday evening news program. The show's producers wanted to film a segment on military leaders who actively contributed to emerging military doctrine, entitled "The New Class of Clausewitzes." Due to the show's popularity, Captain Guy, the commander of all Public Affairs units in the United States Southeast region, contacted Ellie about her participation. A gangly, sunken-chest man with acne scars and greying temples, Guy never left Ellie's side in the days preceding the interview, intently scrutinizing the condition of her ship and crew, the talking points she crafted, and her personal appearance.

"You're exactly what they were hoping to find," Guy informed Ellie. "I told the producers, 'oh yes, Commander

Ellie Apple is the poster girl for the Navy. Couldn't ask for a better representative. But..." Guy trailed off slightly, sitting back in his chair. "They did ask if you were always so... well, um, you look very put together in your official photo."

"I'm not sure I understand what you're suggesting." Ellie said, gritting her teeth, knowing exactly what he suggested.

"Thing is... they, the producers, they want both a warrior and a scholar, you know? Someone rugged... with glasses. Just show up as if you're heading to the ship on a normal day."

Ellie prided herself in looking put together and never set foot anywhere without make-up, even when leading her ship on deployment. She nurtured her vanity, fully aware that her attractiveness contributed to her charisma.

"I'll do my best," Ellie replied, and booked a series of facials and hair appointments in the days leading up to the interview.

While Ellie's actual on-camera interview took two consecutive hours to complete, the entire process lasted for nearly twelve hours, most of which were spent with the show's producers collecting b-roll images, testing potential background shots, and pointing out confidential areas which could not appear on camera. Guy lurked in the background the entire time, visibly flinching at her answers or giving her a gleeful thumbs-up sign in response to others. Ellie ignored him and abandoned the staid talking points Guy had approved as soon the production team started filming.

When the segment finally aired, she appeared on screen for less than three minutes. Other featured officers – a balding Army intelligence Colonel and a barrel-chested Marine Corps Major who worked at Cyber Command – appeared on screen for about ten minutes each.

"You see, Commander, the show producers... had a few... concerns..." Guy's sentences dragged along at a sluggish cadence. Ellie wanted to scream at him to get to the point. "Naturally, the public image of an officer should be one that inspires... authority. They didn't think that's what you projected."

"We all know," Ellie cringed and continued in as steady a tone as she could manage, "the implication here. I'm a woman in command. But didn't you push back?"

"The thing is," Guy fumbled with a stack of blue folders scattered frantically across his desk, digging them out from beneath a heap of crumbled sandwich wrappers and plastic take-out containers. "While the producers recommended the voice modifications, we – the Navy– worried about putting you on screen for so long. We approved the change and... um, actually we're the ones who limited your on-screen time."

"Excuse me?" Ellie sprung forward involuntarily.

Guy started at Ellie's abrupt movement, then composed himself by placing his oversized hand on his chest. "We thought – and the producers agreed – that you came off sounding a bit too... arrogant."

"Arrogant?" She paused a second to allow Guy to explain his assertion. He made no attempt to explain and instead stared back at her vacuously, maneuvering a paperclip around his mouth.

"Sir, how exactly did I come across as arrogant? When I was asked to talk about my work?"

Guy continued to work the paperclip across his mouth. Small saliva bubbles formed in the corner of his mouth and leaked down the paperclip's silver curves.

"That was exactly it. You talked a lot about your work. We wanted the public to see a selfless Naval officer. You know? Someone who really puts the ship first."

"I mentioned our ship's performance frequently," Ellie crossed her arms. "All the others spoke about their work. And there is the difficulty of not talking about yourself when asked. Wasn't that the point?"

She watched Guy's absurdly long fingers flutter through the wrappers and sticky notes littering his keyboard and workspace.

"There was a lot of self-promotion. You said you were a Rhodes Scholar."

"I *was* a Rhodes Scholar."

Guy shrugged. "Still. You didn't have to mention it. This is what they're talking about, you know. Your abra-

siveness really came out on camera"

Ellie opened her mouth to respond, but stood to leave instead.

"There's more..." Guy called out as soon as Ellie reached the door, holding out a paper for her to see. "Does the name Admiral Meleager mean anything to you?"

"My former Commanding Officer? He was my old mentor." Ellie said. She felt her face grow hot. He *was* a mentor, she repeated to herself somewhat less credulously. She picked up the paper and scanned the contents – a printout of an online comment board. The graphics looked simple and grainy, and advertisements for decade-old movies and defunct e-commerce businesses overwhelmed the margins and header space. Among the visual clutter Ellie could discern two important details from the busy page: the title (MilWivesChat.com) and her own name.

Putting this out there for all navy wives to see: lt ellie apple is the bitch who is sleeping with my husband in a sad attempt to try to get ahead. This awful ugly slut lured him in on deployment and after hours keeping him from me and our children. headed to some pentagon job she probably slept her way into. all wardroom wives out there be warned!

Ellie read the message a second time, and a third, in an attempt to make sense of the content. Then she froze, recalling the question about Admiral Meleager.

He had been Commander Meleager then, her ship's commanding officer. He had been the one who encouraged Ellie to start writing, gifting her with the advice that would change the course of her career: "You've got a brain in your head, Apple. Don't let the routine and the rote way we go about things dull that. The Navy needs you to think as much as it needs you to operate."

When he spoke to her, a broad smile stretched across his lightly lined face and nearly reached his temples. He started greying during that tour, Ellie remembered. He came onboard looking so young and vibrant. Toward the end of his command, he appeared more refined, the nascent grey hairs highlighting softening sharp features.

His hair had grayed completely now, Ellie thought,

remembering the last official picture she saw of him online. He now possessed the dignified countenance of an authoritative leader, both stern and warm, intelligent and humble. Still as objectively handsome as he had been fifteen years ago.

"This is slanderous and immature. Not to mention unfounded. But how exactly does this affect what happened with the news coverage?" Ellie asked, shaking her head in disbelief. A day ago, she thought the news segment portended an ambitious turn for her future. Today, she felt as if she fell through a trap door leading to her past.

Voices involuntarily bobbed to the surface in her mind, insecurities and invectives resurrected from long ago.

"You know the only reason she was ranked as the top junior officer on the ship is because of her relationship with the captain." A small group of officers assigned to the ship with Ellie congregated outside of the Executive Officer's stateroom, right above a ladder-well. She intended to ascend the ladder and join the group, but paused as she heard the comment.

"Shhh..." Another officer cautioned, still unaware of her presence. "The Exec's in there."

"Oh, to hell with him," another said. "He knows they're fucking. We all do."

She wanted to remember her response with pride – how she stormed up the ladder and through the gaggle, demanding they shut their mouths, laying out her accolades one by one, pointing out the myriad examples of how she worked harder and longer and more intelligently than they ever did.

But none of that actually occurred.

Ellie remained at the foot of the ladder and only ascended once they all disbanded. She had heard stories of angry women, the bitches and the harpies. That would not be her story.

Instead, she endured the whispers she heard when she entered rooms on the ship with an air of moral superiority. *Let them all be wrong*, she thought, delighting in their pettiness as she channeled her thoughts into her writing, advanced in her career, and tried not to notice the cold receptions she received from her male colleagues. It hadn't been since her most recent tour as commanding officer, almost seventeen years since she received her commission, that she felt comfortable showing her natural warmth. Her newly gained position finally granted her permission to be open and agreeable without her motives being questioned.

When she recalled her chats with Commander Meleager now, she wanted to believe she acted professionally, that she never smiled coquettishly or lowered her head. Ellie worked hard to strip herself of the girlish habits conditioned into her from childhood and comport herself as more solid and assertive, plucking out every demure and conceding fiber from her body.

Yet her memory was a congenital liar. She most likely giggled, made her voice higher, and conceded on points she wished she had doggedly defended. No amount of wishing otherwise could alter that fact. Still, neither she nor Commander Meleager crossed any lines. Ellie remembered the stories she heard of women who slept with senior officers – homewreckers who slept their way to the top. That would not be her story.

"As you know, there have been quite a few... embarrassments for the military in the past decade involving women and their superiors... Shameful stuff. Naturally, we try as hard as possible to... prevent this type of exposure." Guy's slimy voice jolted Ellie back to the present.

"I- I can't believe this," Ellie stammered. The words felt vacant, as if her ability to process language deteriorated with her growing consternation. "All of this, this, effort, this censorship, because of one ridiculous comment on an obscure site? From over 15 years ago?"

Guy cleared his throat. "Well, that's not all. You see, we, the Navy Public Affairs Office, that is... Well, we're of the opinion that we were remiss in... granting you that interview to begin with."

"What?" Ellie felt something lurch inside of her chest, as if Guy's comment awoke some dormant creature slumbering inside her.

"You see, we found this... unfortunate online artifact a little too late. We were too excited for the nationwide coverage and skipped our normal due diligence. But, once we found it, we had to engage in... damage control. *Weekly World* was making final edits, so we couldn't have them remove you outright, but we did ask them to scale back your screen time."

"Because of petty rumors?"

"We're protecting you. Saving you from being publicly humiliated.

"The public could care less."

"Wrong!" Guy bellowed, pointing his bony finger into the air and straightening his back. "I'm sure you think so, off in your brainy little world of books and research and whatnot. The rest of us? We love it when an attractive woman is sleeping with a powerful married man. Who cares about what you've accomplished? The world needs a villain, preferably one who thinks she's smarter and better than the rest of us. This is why," Guy concluded. "This is why we can no longer allow you to publish articles as long as you remain on active duty. You're too much of a liability."

"What?" Ellie felt a hot, suffocating sensation slowly creep over her face and down her neck. It proceeded down her spine, slowly, painfully, making her recoil like a defensive animal prepared to strike out violently in search of a desperate escape.

"The decision is final, I'm sorry to say. The Department of the Navy has... ah, here it is, imposed a publication blackout on you. As long as you're with the Navy, you won't be allowed to submit any articles, opinion pieces – anything – without punitive action and dismissal. Here's the signed order."

"You can't..." Ellie protested. Her arms and legs throbbed. She attempted to remain calm, but felt as if her body were governed by some vicious, leonine urge to tear apart everything within her view. "My writing, I've done hours of research, all in service to the Navy, for God's sake, to expand what we think is possible. My work matters. They can't just tell me not to do it."

Guy shifted uncomfortably in his seat again. "We can, as long as you remain in the Navy. The order, you see, was signed by, um...." He handed the form he held in his hand to Ellie.

She didn't have to read the typed name to recognize the signature: Admiral Thomas F. Meleager.

"So, this is how it is. Perception wins. The men in charge protect themselves." Ellie felt her throat tickle, as if to suppress her urge to roar in fury. Inside her chest, the clawing rage continued. It lurked within her, animal-like, desperately seeking the scent of blood after years of lying dormant. This urge, Ellie realized, would transform her.

"Commander Apple," Guy replied. "Wake up. That's how it is... That's how it's always been."

Ellie suddenly lurched toward Guy. One hand landed

flat on the desk then clenched, crumbling all the paper-work underneath. She thrust her other hand toward Guy's face, resisting the urge to claw at his eyes.

"You," she growled. "All of you. You'd rather I be turned into some kind of monster than see me succeed." In one swift motion, she flung all the detritus littering Guy's desk to the floor and bounded out of his office.

It had rained while Ellie met with Captain Guy, a quick and violent convective summer deluge which drenched the sunbaked pavement for a half-hour, then enveloped the bright afternoon in a damp, steamy cloud, fragrant with the odors of asphalt, rotting clams, and diesel fuel. Even though Ellie only had to walk a half mile from the building back to her ship, the humidity caused her chin-length, dark blonde hair to frizz and circle her head in a wanton mane.

As she padded along the waterfront, Ellie felt an intense anger metastasize underneath her skin, a metamor-phosis causing her entire body to radiate fury. Her knuck-les cramped under the force of her own exertion until they knotted and balled up without assistance, like two paws. Her breath grew increasingly shallow and she actively willed herself to cry, praying for some release from the rage that enveloped her. Tears evaded her. Ellie remembered the stories she had heard about the women who would cry when faced with disappointment. That would not be her story.

Her story, Ellie now realized, was something else en-tirely. It finally caught up with her.

Once she arrived at her ship, Ellie stormed past the quarterdeck and toward her stateroom, streaking by the officers who lined up along the narrow passageway to greet her, checking one against the side of the bulkhead with a strength she never knew she possessed and knock-ing an outstretched folder to the floor in the process. She slammed the door behind her, leaving her officers and their perplexed, gawking faces in her wake.

The calm inside her stateroom only aggravated her more. The accolades she hung upon her walls appeared to taunt her – her commissioning certificate and framed award she won as class salutatorian, a picture of her shaking the president's hand in uniform, her diploma magna cum laude, the college track medals, her Officer of the Year award, the plaque she received from the Arte-mis Foundation, signed images of ships where she spent previous tours – they represented nothing more than tantalizing mirages, unrealized promises cast in bronze. She shrieked and ripped down every framed image and gilded crest, throwing them against the bulkheads and creating a metallic, chaotic din. When every oak-weighted, glass-gar-nished acknowledgement of her adult life lay scattered on the floor in pieces picked up the shards and flung them, too, then paced across the room and over the debris like an animal caged.

A sharp knock interrupted her fury: "Ma'am, are you OK?"

She roared back in reply.

"My god," she heard someone say over the crash of hurled objects and the shuffle of feet scurrying from her door.

"Has she lost it?" One of her officers asked.

"She's a monster," Another whispered.

Ellie bared her teeth, recalling her parting words to Guy.

"Yes," she growled. "Yes I am." 🄼

Contributors

Virginia Betts

Virginia has a degree in Literature, and a postgraduate degree in teaching English. She now runs a tuition business. She is a passionate advocate for neuro-diversity, particularly as she is autistic. She has had poems, articles and stories published and broadcast on BBC Radio, and is currently writing for a professional theatre production. Her collection of short stories, *The Camera Obscure*, will be published in late 2021; writing is her preferred method of emotional expression. *Dysmorphic* deals with the seemingly irrational feelings surrounding body dysmorphia, and wider themes surrounding female roles, identity, and relationships. *Natasha* and *Stepping Out On Derby Day* are both inspired by true events almost a century apart. Virginia is married with one son, and her passions, apart from words, are swimming and playing the violin.

Emily Bowles

As we all relearn what it means to retreat into our homes, I have thought about the ways in which oscillating metaphors and realities of motherhood shape us--and how the domestic space is a dizzying nexus of disorder. My poems about Margaret Cavendish for this issue address themes I visit in my chapbooks *(His Journal, My Stella* and *The Satisfactory Nothing of Girls)*, and they recover her as an example of how multifarious women can be: she is both a literary foremother and not a mother, someone removed from canons and rewritten as strange, impossible, absurd.

Abby Brunt

Abby Brunt is a poet and licensed massage therapist. Her work often explores themes of family, brokenness and survival. She has an MFA in Poetry from Old Dominion University. She grew up in a fundamentalist evangelical church where women were expected to be silent, submit to men and have as many babies as possible. Learning about women's rights and suffrage was an important part of claiming her voice and in breaking out of that worldview. These poems speak to that experience and to the lives of women still living under the oppression of these fundamentalist churches.

Susan Caggiano

Susan Caggiano teaches writing at Santa Monica College and has returned to her writing practice after raising her daughter and reimagining life after motherhood. She loves travel, hiking and the outdoors and sees her writing as both craft and life buoy. She has poetry published in *The Northridge Review Retrospective* and is currently working on personal essays and a memoir. "Shift" was inspired by the theme of working class family relationships, and in particular, the effects on her father and his relationship with her.

Jillian Danback-McGhan

Jillian Danback-McGhan is a writer and former Naval Officer. Her work most recently appears in *Line of Advance* and *Deadly Writer's Patrol* and has been anthologized in *Our Best War Stories* by Middle West Press. She is the winner of the 2020 Col. Darren L. Wright Memorial Writing award and is currently working on a collection of short fiction. She lives in Annapolis, MD with her family.

Debra Madaris Efird

Debra Madaris Efird, from Harrisburg, NC, is a writer who has always championed women's causes but became adamantly political in recent years. She has participated in women's marches, attended protests, contacted members of Congress over 3000 times, and even made those annoying phone calls to get out the vote. She is author of "Groups in Practice: A School Counselor's Collection" (Routledge 2012). Other credits include saturdayeveningpost.com, livinglutheran.org, and numerous anthologies, magazines, and professional journals.

Nancy Johnson

Nancy Johnson lives with her life partner on a lake in the Canadian Shield, about 200 miles north of Toronto, Canada. She's been writing short stories for some time but has recently been making more effort to share them with the world. A proudly second-wave feminist, she believes it was not just the large, dramatic events that drove progress toward women's equality. Countless smaller moments of epiphany and personal acts of courage in the post WWII era, also propelled us forward. "Matters of Credit" is a story about one of those moments.

Rosalind Kaplan

Rosalind Kaplan has been published in several literary and medical journals, including *Amarillo Bay, Annals of Internal Medicine, Another Chicago Magazine, Brandeis Magazine, Eastern Iowa Review, HerSTRY, Minerva Rising, Prompted, a Philadelphia Stories Anthology,* and *The Pulse Magazine.* She is a physician and also teaches narrative medicine and medical memoir writing at Thomas Jefferson University/Sidney Kimmel Medical College. Dr. Kaplan is a 2020 graduate of Lesley University's MFA in creative nonfiction, and she has attended a number of writing workshops. She lives with her husband and a rescue dog, and has two grown children.

Paula Rudnick

Paula is a former TV producer whose credits range from late night Rock and Roll to Emmy-nominated movies. Her poems have been published in *Halfway Down the Stairs, Moon Magazine, Poets Magazine* and included in anthologies from Darkhouse Books and Constellations. When not writing, cooking, Zooming or sanitizing in 2020, Paula Rudnick devoted herself to political work. Happy 2021!

Lee Reilly

I'm the author of two nonfiction books, and several dozen articles and essays. My fiction and nonfiction have been recognized by Illinois Arts Council, the Barbara Deming award, Hunger Mountain, and other publications and arts organizations. Other Rosaleen stories have appeared in Quarter After Eight, London Independent Story Prize, Hypertext, and utxt3 by Medusa's Laugh Press. Voting is voice, and writing is voice, and the real Rosaleen, my grandmother, treasured both.

Deborah Schmedemann

After thirty-five decades in the legal profession, most of them as a law professor, Deborah Schmedemann now volunteers with newcomers to the United States and particularly enjoys teaching adult English language learners. She has published essays in the anthologies *Surprised by Joy; Corners: Voices on Change; Awake in the World;* and *Home: An Anthology of Minnesota Fiction, Memoir and Poetry.* She lives as close as one can get to the Mississippi River in south Minneapolis, yet is often found with her two daughters and their families in the Chicago area or traveling internationally with her husband.

Kay Smith-Blum

Kay Smith-Blum, Woman Business Owner (NWWA) of the Year (2013) is a recovering retailer, living in Seattle. "Desco Drive" is the short story that beget her second novel of historical fiction, now out for agent review. Her short stories can be found at CommuterLit.com, *Fiction Attic Press, Fiction Southeast* (late 2021) and *The Stray Branch* (2022). Her humorous essays (nominated for Best of the Net) may be found at *Pif Magazine, Heavy Feather Review, The Furious Gazelle, Quail Bell Magazine, Bewildering Stories* and *Down in the Dirt Magazine* (2020 Anthology). Twitter: @kaysmithblum; Instagram: @discerningKSB; www.KaySmith-Blum.com

Karin Spitfire

Karin Spitfire is the author of *Standing with Trees* and a chapbook "Wild Caught." Her poem "Liquidation" won the national first place in the 2019 Joe Gouveia Outermost Poetry Contest, sponsored by WOMR, Provincetown. "What is to be Offered published in The Kerf, was nominated for a Pushcart Prize. She was the Poet Laureate of Belfast, Me in 2007 & 2008. Spitfire, dancer, poet, artist, credits radical intersectional feminist activism, the rocky coast of Maine for tenderizing/healing her fierce abused edges.

Violet Snow

Violet Snow is a journalist and the author of *To March or to Marry,* a recently published historical novel about suffrage and women's clubs. Violet's articles have appeared in the *New York Times* "Disunion" blog, *Civil War Times, American Ancestors, Woodstock Times, Jewish Currents,* and many other periodicals. Her fiction and memoir have been published in *Otter Magazine, Pilgrimage, Tinker Street,* and the podcast series "The Strange Recital." She lives in upstate New York.

Lisa Zimmerman

Lisa Zimmerman poetry collections include *How the Garden Looks from Here* (winner of the Violet Reed Haas Poetry Award), *The Light at the Edge of Everything* (Anhinga Press) and The Hours I Keep (Main Street Rag). Her chapbook *Sainted* is forthcoming (Main Street Rag, 2021). Her poetry and fiction have appeared in *Redbook, The Sun, Poet Lore, Colorado Review, Cave Wall, Amethyst Review, Florida Review, SWWIM Every Day* and other journals. Her poems have been nominated for Best of the Net, five times for the Pushcart Prize, and included in the 2020 *Best Small Fictions* anthology. She lives with her husband in Fort Collins, Colorado and is a Professor of English and creative writing at the University of Northern Colorado.

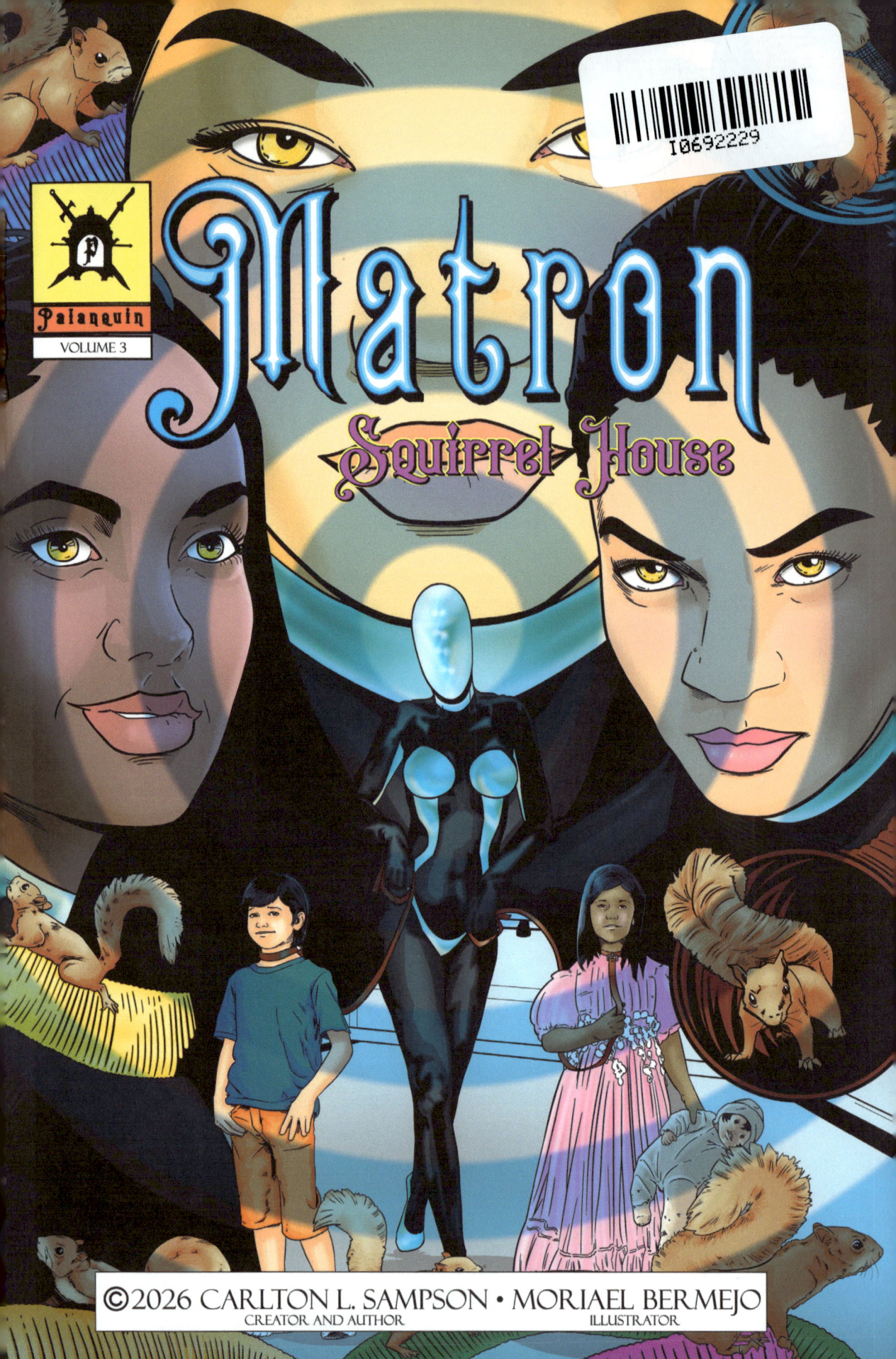

MALE DOMINANCE IS COMMON
IN MANY HUMAN CULTURES
AND IN SOME SPECIES.

HOWEVER, HUMAN FAMILY
STRUCTURES HAVE CHANGED.

RESOURCES FOR PROVIDING DAILY
SUSTENANCE ARE ABUNDANT.

WHERE IS WENDY?
IN THE HOUSE.

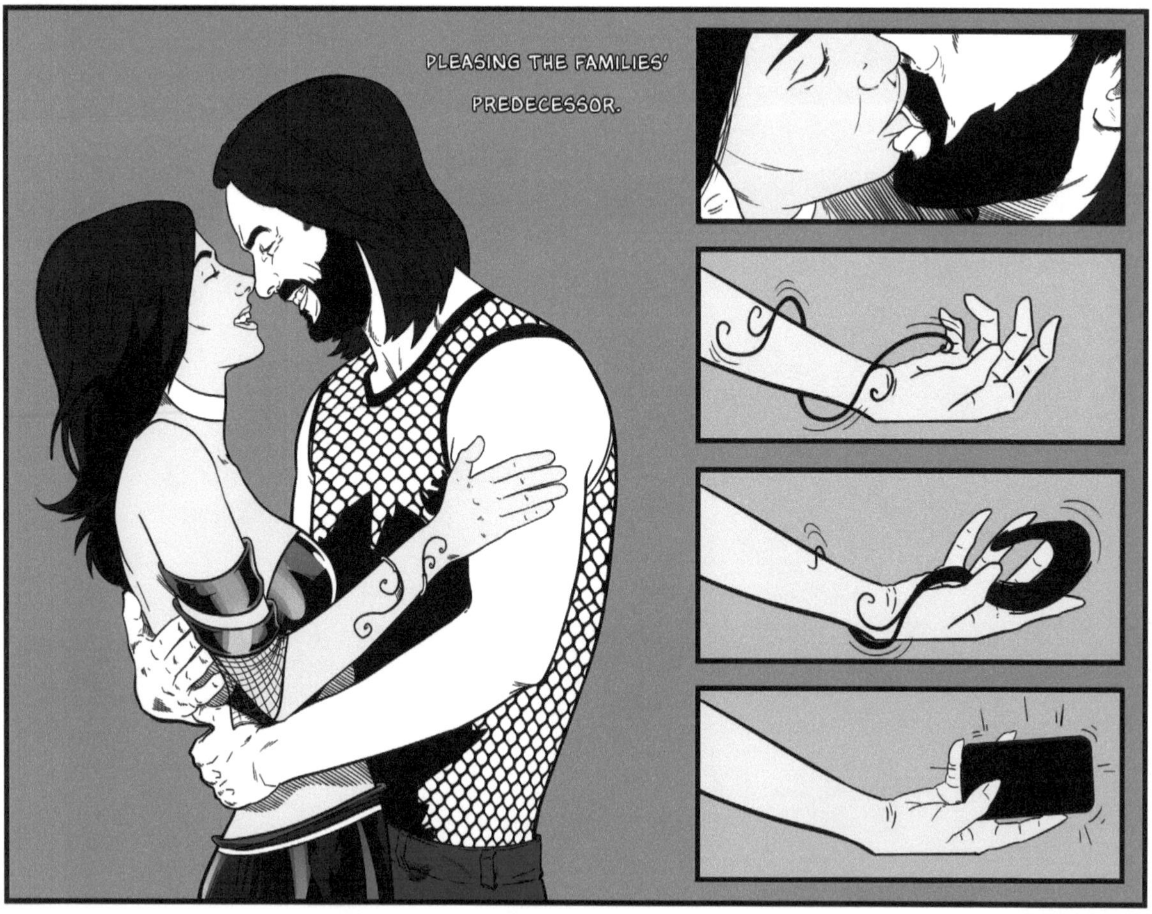
PLEASING THE FAMILIES'
PREDECESSOR.

ALEIRABA IS HEARTBROKEN AGAIN. sigh
ALEIRABA! ARIELLE CALLED ME. SHE SAID ADEL PICKED YOU UP IN NEWARK.
YES. I KNEW THEY WOULD BE PASSING. SO I–
sigh SHE LOVES GETTING ATTACHED.

JUST STAY AWAY FROM MY DAUGHTER, ALEIRABA.
I NEEDED A RIDE, ANNA!

A RIDE? SO YOU COULD DO THIS TERRIBLE THING IN FLORIDA AS WELL. MURDER IS A SIN!
ANNA, IF ARIELLE HAD NOT CALLED YOU, YOU WOULD NOT KNOW OR CARE.

SHE WAS IN TEARS! ARIELLE DOES NOT NEED TO SHARE IN YOUR UGLINESS.
ARIELLE WILL BE OKAY, ANNA. ≠sigh≠ SHE HAS—
GWEN! YES!

WOW! MY GOD! IT IS YOU!
SURPRISE!
WENDY! ≥h-!!≤
ARIELLE HAS ADEL. THEY ARE MEANT FOR EACH OTHER.
Food

THEN JUST STAY AWAY FROM HER, ALEIRABA!
SO, DEFIANT. ≥ha ha≤ YOU AND ARIELLE ARE SO MUCH ALIKE. ≥ha, ha≤ YOUR GRANDDAUGHTER WILL BE IMPOSSIBLE. ≥hmm, yum≤

WAIT! WHAT? MY ARIELLE? PREGNANT?
NOT YET, BUT SOON, ANNA. SOON.

ALEIRABA! LET'S MEET HERE BEFORE THE FESTIVAL!
THANK YOU, ALEIRABA!
MEET BEFORE? OKAY. BUT MARTINIQUE. NOT PATMOS. I'VE GOT TO GO. ≠b-y-e≠
MARTINIQUE. MATRON IS HOMESICK.

I DREAMED ABOUT YOU LAST NIGHT.
a-w-w
YOU ARE SO, SWEET.
WE BOTH DID.

ha ha
GILL, YOU ARE A LIAR. HE DID NOT DREAM ABOUT ME LAST NIGHT. BUT, GILL DID SENSE MY PRESENCE WHEN I–
JUST A QUICK FROLIC.
NO GWEN! NO PRESENCE.

NO. NO QUICK FROLIC. UNFORTUNATELY, WE HAVE GUESTS COMING FOR A BARBEQUE.
HOW LONG ARE YOU STAYING THIS TIME, GWEN?
JUST THE NIGHT.

I HAD A DELIVERY IN DENVER. YOU WERE CLOSE SO I TOOK A FREE DAY.
THEN ON TO MARTINIQUE.
WHAT A JOB. I'M JEALOUS.

AS A PALANQUIN COURIER I'VE MADE SOME WEALTHY FRIENDS.
YOUR FRIEND ANNA WAS MAD ABOUT YOU MEDDLING WITH ARIELLE.

ANNA ALWAYS ACCUSES ME OF INFLUENCING HER DAUGHTER.
DO YOU INFLUENCE HER DAUGHTER?

≹snicker≶ ARIELLE ACCUSES ME OF INFLUENCING HER MOTHER. I GET IT FROM BOTH SIDES. I AM JUST THEIR MEDIUM.

YOU DO KNOW MORE ABOUT ARIELLE HAVING A BABY THAN HER MOTHER, ANNA, DOES.

WILL YOU MEDDLE IN HER GRANDDAUGHTER'S LIFE AS WELL?

NO DOUBT.

≹chuckle≶

DOES ADEL KNOW ABOUT ARIELLE'S EXPECTED PREGNANCY?
giggle
NO, BUT I DO. AND I WAS RIGHT ABOUT YOU TWO.
SHE WAS RIGHT ABOUT US, WENDY.

IS THAT WHY THEY CALL YOU GODMOTHER?
IT IS MY NICKNAME BECAUSE I MEDDLE SO MUCH.
EXCUSE ME.
OF COURSE.

EXCUSE ME, ALEIRABA. YOU REQUESTED NOTIFICATION. THE KERNS SAMPLE HAS ARRIVED. CONGRATULATIONS ON YOUR FLORIDA KILL.
ACKNOWLEDGED. SCHEDULE ANNA AND HER SISTERS IN MARTINIQUE BEFORE THE PATMOS REUNION.

MARTINIQUE, ACKNOWLEDGED, ALEIRABA.
FLORIDA WAS A LOT OF FUN. THE KILL WAS NOT AS DISTASTEFUL AS I EXPECTED.
KERNS? FLORIDA KILL?
GILL, DON'T ASK.

I AM DELAYED HERE A DAY.
GWEN'S ETA?
HER DENVER DELAY.
ONE OF HER FAVORED FAMILIES.
GWEN'S ETA GROUND-ZERO 65 MINUTES.
MARTINIQUE.
ALEIRABA IS HOMESICK.

GWEN, WAS YOUR FLORIDA KILL ANNA'S FLORIDA MURDER?
NEXT QUESTION!
YES, GILL. WHEN I WAS IN FLORIDA I COMMITTED MURDER, MORE OR LESS.

YOU MORE OR LESS MURDERED SOMEONE IN FLORIDA? GWEN, ARE YOU AN ASSASSIN?
SHE JUST DELIVERS MESSAGES FOR THE RICH GLOBALLY, GILL.
Ǝha haƐ I WAS ALLIGATOR HUNTING IN FLORIDA.

ANNA IS A VEGAN. ANNA HEAVILY FUNDS ANIMAL RIGHTS ORGANIZATIONS. Ǝha haƐ SO, WHERE IS MY BEAUTIFUL LITTLE NAMESAKE?
Ǝha haƐ GWEN IS ON LEAVE. SHE WILL BE HOME SOON.
Ǝha haƐ WE HAVE ABOUT AN HOUR.

WHO— WHAT ARE YOU?

WHY DO WE LOVE— WANT YOU SO MUCH? WHY DO WE FEEL—

WHY DO WE KNOW WE BELONG TO YOU, GWEN?

YOU BELONG TO EACH OTHER. I AM JUST YOUR MEDIUM.

GOOD NEWS, SIR. WE HAVE CONFIRMATION OF THE *FILLETTE* PHOTO IMAGE.
EYEWITNESSES?
YES, SIR. A COUPLE TRANSIENTS. ACCORDING TO THE EYEWITNESSES THE YACHT ARRIVED BEFORE THE RIDER ARRIVED.

THEN IT WAS A RENDEZVOUS. ARE YOU CONFIDENT YOUR EYE-WITNESSES ARE RELIABLE? THEY ARE TRANSIENTS.
YES. THEY WERE CONFIRMED AS KNOWN TRANSIENTS WITH AREA BUSINESS OWNERS.

ACCORDING TO WITNESSES, THE BLUR IS A MOTORCYCLE AND FEMALE RIDER STANDING ON THE DOCK. SHE WAS WEARING A BLACK AND BLUE JUMPSUIT AND BLUE HELMET.
HMM, A PALANQUIN COURIER'S JUMPSUIT PERHAPS? ADEL FEISAL'S FIFTH WIFE, ARIELLE SAIGH, IS A FORMER LOVER OF MATRON ORNEY.
THE MATRON?

YES. FULL NAME MATRON SAIGH-ORNEY. OWNER AND CHIEF OF SECURITY AT ORNEY WINES. PARENT COMPANY OF PALANQUIN CHAUFFEURS' TRAVEL MANAGEMENT.
AKA, MATRON. A 26-YEAR-OLD OVERTLY LIBIDINOUS MULTI-BILLIONAIRE ADVENTURER.
SHE IS ALSO A PART-TIME PROFESSIONAL MOTORCYCLE RACER. MATRON OCCASIONALLY RACES BUT ALWAYS WINS.

MATRON WEARS A PALANQUIN COURIER'S JUMPSUIT WHEN SHE RACES.
THE SAIGH-ORNEY FINANCIAL DYNASTY STARTED IN 1537. THE YEAR AMAR SAIGH AND VAGABOND ORNEY CHARTERED THE TRIPOLI TRADING SLAVE-TRADING COMPANY.
TRIPOLI TRADING SLAVE-TRADING COMPANY?

THE COMPANY MILITIA BECAME PALANQUIN CHAUFFEURS IN 1860.
MATRON IS BLACK.

THE SAIGH-ORNEY FAMILY IS OF INDO-ARAB AND FRENCH DESCENT. THE FAMILY IS LARGE, MULTI-RACIAL, AND LED BY A SECRETIVE MATRIARCHY.
SECRETIVE? A WHITE TWELVE-YEAR-OLD MATRON ORNEY MADE THE HEADLINES IN 1917.

SHE WAS SOLE BENEFICIARY OF INDUSTRIALIST JOHN HAMMOND'S WILL AND WON A LAWSUIT FILED AGAINST HER BY HIS FAMILY.
WOW. DURING THE TRIAL, MULTIPLE HAMMOND FAMILY MEMBERS JEALOUSLY CONFESSED HAVING SEXUAL RELATIONS WITH DEFENDANT MATRON ORNEY.

SHE WAS THE FIRST, AND UNTIL NOW, ONLY PUBLICLY IDENTIFIED SAIGH-ORNEY FAMILY MATRIARCH.
BECAUSE MATRON IS BLACK, I NEVER CONNECTED HER TO THE HAMMOND TRIAL. DAMN.

THE SAIGH-ORNEY MULTI-NATIONAL CONGLOMERATE HAS THE RESOURCES TO PRODUCE ADVANCED WEAPONRY.
IN 1932, PALANQUIN CHAUFFEURS EXTERMINATED AN ENTIRE CRIMINAL ORGANIZATION FOR KILLING ONE OF ITS EMPLOYEES.

*MIA; Miami International Aitport.

ELECTROCUTIONS AND MELTED WINDOWS CONNECT THE AMF AND WHITE SHARKS CRIME SCENES. ARE WE RETRACTING OUR STATEMENT ON MIKE KERNS' INNOCENCE?
NO RETRACTION, SIR.

THERE IS NO EVIDENCE CONNECTING MIKE KERNS TO HUMAN TRAFFICKING OR ORGAN HARVESTING IN HIS NEWARK AMF FACILITIES.
WHAT ABOUT THE 15 BODIES IDENTIFIED SO FAR, OF THE 85 BODIES RECOVERED FROM THE AMF CRIME SCENES?

THEY WERE ALL FOREIGN NATIONAL MERCENARIES. FIVE OF THEM FORMER ISS EMPLOYEES.
THE CAPTAIN OF *C. S. TOLERANCE* HIRED THE CREW. THE AMF ABATTOIR MANAGER HIRED THE SECURITY. THEY BOTH DIED IN THE ASSAULTS.

WE ASSUME AMF PERSONNEL KNEW OR TRUSTED THEIR ASSAILANTS. BOTH FACILITIES WERE INFILTRATED AND OVERCOME FROM WITHIN.
A SEXTING PARTNER OF THE VICTIMS AND SURVIVORS. YESTERDAY THE FIRST TIME THEY HAD SEEN OR MET.
FBI

POLICE
NEWS
FN
WHAT ELSE DO WE KNOW ABOUT SUSPECT, EL, AKA LADY LIBERTY 2013? IS EL RESPONSIBLE FOR BRONSON'S EXECUTION? ALLIGATORS ATE KERNS. WHY DID THE WOMEN SURVIVE?
WE ARE WAITING FOR THE NEXT PHASE LAWYERS AND DOCTORS TO GRANT ACCESS TO THE WHITE SHARKS SURVIVORS.
FEDERAL BUREAU OF INVESTIGATION
CLASSIFIED
CASE FILE
CROCODILE ATTACKS
EVENT SUMMARY
EVIDENCE

ENROUTE TO THE HOSPITAL, THEY IMPLICATED KERNS' AND BRONSON'S RESPONSIBILITY FOR THE 14 OTHER EXECUTIONS.
THE CONDITION OF KERNS' REMAINS SUGGESTS AN OINTMENT OR INSERTED LURE. POSSIBLY SONIC.

IMAGES DISCOVERED IN KERNS' RESIDENCE SUGGEST THERE IS EVIDENCE ON HIS ENCRYPTED CLOUD STORAGE.
MY COMMAND DISPATCHED FORENSIC AND CRYPTANALYTIC SPECIALISTS TO THE FLORIDA MORTUARY AND CRIME SCENE TO ASSIST.

GOVERNOR BUCKET WANTS TO MAKE A STATEMENT ON MIKE KERNS. WHAT CAN I TELL HIM ABOUT THIS INVESTIGATION?
TELL GOVERNOR BUCKET, KERNS AND BRONSON ARE SUSPECTED OF FEMICIDAL ATROCITIES AND WERE MURDERED. AT PRESENT, THERE IS NO MOTIVE AND ONE ELUSIVE SUSPECT FOR THEIR MURDERS.

THEN THE OVERALL POPULATION IS CONDITIONED BY REPEATED SOUND AND IMAGE PATTERNS.
YES, THEN FOCUSED MESSAGING METHODS FOR SELECT SEGMENTS OF THE POPULATION.

SEGMENTATION BASED ON DESIRED PHYSICAL CHARACTERISTICS AND GENETIC NORMS OF FAMILY GROUPS.
EXACTLY, FAMILY GROUP NORMS. UH-AUNT GWEN, I KNOW ABOUT YOU THREE.

I HAVE ALWAYS KNOWN ABOUT YOU THREE. JUST A FEELING.
YOU ARE PART OF A BEAUTIFUL FAMILY, GWEN.

YOU GUYS ARE ONE OF MY FAVORITE FAMILIES.
I THOUGHT I WAS YOUR DAUGHTER FOR A WHILE. *giggle*

AUNT GWEN—NO!
ha ha NO. NO KIDS, JUST PETS—OW!

WHITE-FACED CARNIVOROUS MUTANT BASTARDS BIT ME.
SORRY, I SHOULD HAVE WARNED YOU ABOUT THEM, THAT BREED SOONER.

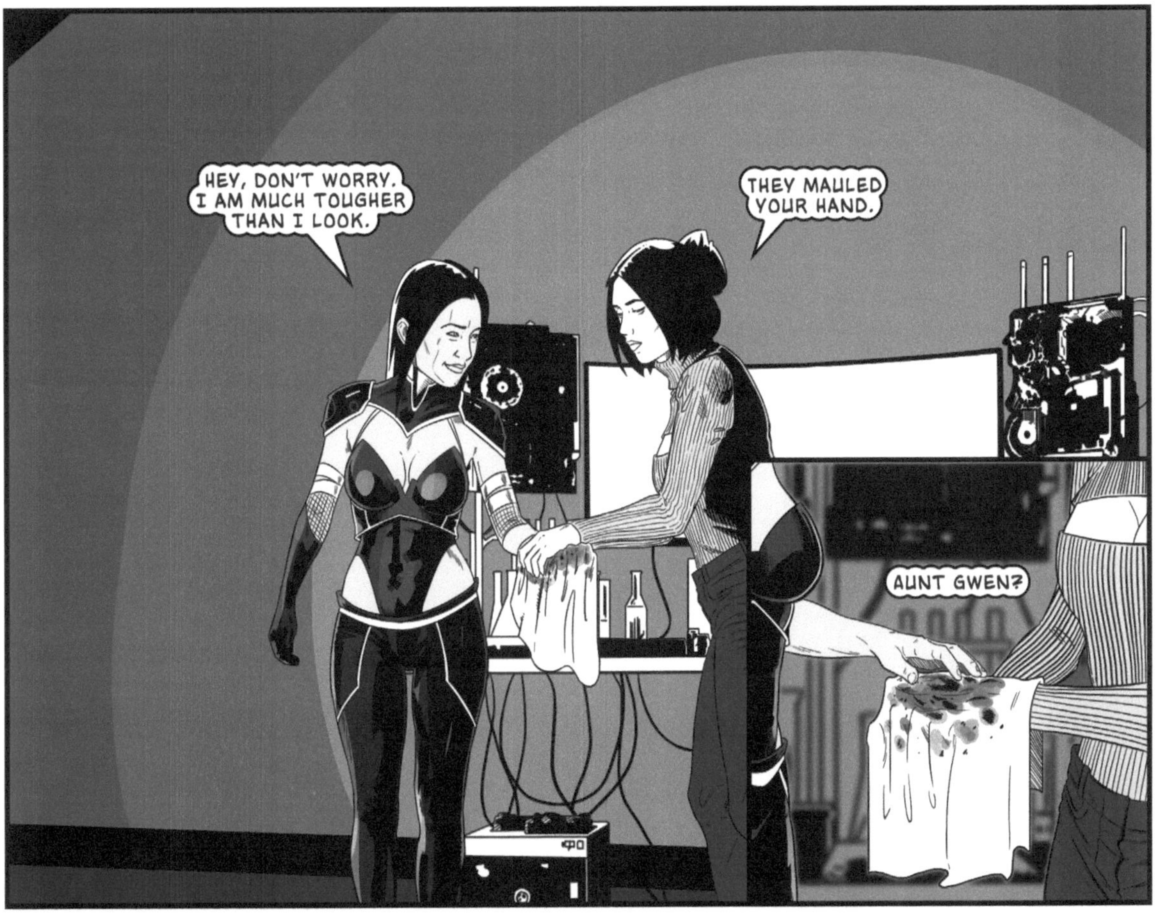
HEY, DON'T WORRY. I AM MUCH TOUGHER THAN I LOOK.
THEY MAULED YOUR HAND.
AUNT GWEN?

WHY ARE THESE WHITE-FACED TREE SQUIRRELS SO HOSTILE?
THEY ARE HYBRIDS. CONDITIONED TO BE SEXUALLY AGGRESSIVE, TERRITORIAL, INVASIVE, AND VIOLENT IF INVADED.

GWEN, WHY DID YOU BREED A STRAIN OF PREDACIOUS TREE SQUIRRELS?
I BRED THE STRAIN IN PREPARATION OF SHUTTING THE SQUIRREL HOUSE DOWN ONE DAY.

THE WHITE-FACED STRAIN COMPENSATES FOR INBRED DOCILITY AND SQUIRREL HOUSE DOMESTICATION.
YOUR PRIMARY POPULATION NEEDED PREDACIOUS TRAITS TO SURVIVE IN THE WILD.

YES. AND IT'S EVIDENT, MY SQUIRRELS HAVE SURVIVED, AND FEWER HYBRIDS RETURN WHEN I COME HOME.
THEN YOUR HYBRID INTERBREEDING IS SUCCESSFULLY BREEDING OUT YOUR MUTATIONS.

EXCEPT IN THE MUTANT DOCILE STRAIN, I BRED TO RESPOND TO DAD. THEY LIVE IN AND AROUND THE SQUIRREL HOUSE.
GILL WAS IN HERE FEEDING HIS FAMILY OF SQUIRRELS WHEN I PULLED UP.

THE WHITE-FACE AND THEIR HYBRID OFFSPRING RETURNING WHEN I AM HOME ON LEAVE FROM THE BBC WAS UNEXPECTED.
GILL'S MUTANTS PUT THE WORD OUT YOU'RE HOME.

HOME ON LEAVE. GWEN, THE BROWN BAG CORPORATION IS A CULTIC MISOGYNISTIC ORGANIZATION.
AUNT GWEN, MY RESUME WAS REPEATEDLY REJECTED BECAUSE OF MISOGYNISTIC JEALOUSY, IGNORANCE, AND FEAR OF MY AGE.

THEY FEAR WHAT YOU ARE, WHAT YOU MIGHT KNOW. THEY FEEL, AND ARE INFERIOR.
REGARDLESS, BBC PROVIDES RESOURCES FOR MY RESEARCH AND I RETAIN MY PATENT RIGHTS.

IN RETURN I GET PAID TO WORK ON THEIR PROJECTS. FAIR EXCHANGE.
BUT YOU WORK AND LIVE IN A TOP SECURITY COMPOUND ISOLATED FOR MONTHS.

ONLY FOR NINE MORE MONTHS, UNLESS I RENEW. BBC IS JUST PROTECTING ITS ASSETS.
ASSETS? YOU HAVE SOLD YOURSELF TO CORPORATE INTEREST FOR PERSONAL GAIN. RENEW WITH BBC.
SEE HOW MUCH LONGER YOU ARE JUST DEVELOPING SYNTHETIC ORGANS?
I RESEARCHED PALANQUIN, OBSESSED WITH YOU. YOU HAVE SOLD YOURSELF TO SAIGH-ORNEY CORPORATE CONGLOMERATE AND FAMILY INTERESTS FOR LIFE.
YOU ARE A SPY!

NO, I AM JUST AN EXECUTIVE COURIER WITH A GREAT PENSION PLAN.
AUNT GWEN, I APPLIED TO SAIGH-ORNEY. THEY DID NOT RESPOND.

AUNT GWEN, I NEED YOUR HELP.
OKAY. DON'T RENEW. PALANQUIN WILL CALL.
SUCH A BEAUTIFUL FAMILY.

JACK, IF THEY ARE LOOKING FOR WITNESSES, THE YACHT AVOIDED DETECTION.
I'LL LOOK INTO IT.

WHEN WILL FLORIDA FBI BE ALLOWED TO INTERVIEW THE SURVIVORS?
TOMORROW, I'D IMAGINE. THEY ARE TELLING THE GIRLS ABOUT MIKE TODAY.

OUR LAWYERS ARE WORKING ON SUPPRESSING ANYTHING THE GIRLS SAID IN THE AMBULANCE.
"THE SURVIVORS SHOULD GIVE TRUTHFUL DETAILED INTERVIEWS TO FLORIDA FBI."

DRISCOL OR HARRIS MIGHT REVEAL SOMETHING TO ME ALONE IN A PRIVATE CONVERSATION.
I UNDERSTAND. HEY HONEY! TELL THEM LAWYERS TO HAVE MIKE'S GIRLS GIVE DETAILED, HONEST INTERVIEWS TO THE FBI, SO WE CAN HAVE THE AGENCY WORKING ON THIS.

THE AGENCY IDED 5 ISS EX-EMPLOYEES. AMONGST THE BODIES RECOVERED AT THE AMF CRIME SCENES. ALL FOREIGN NATIONALS.
FIVE MORE BODIES WILL IDENTIFY AS ISS EX-EMPLOYEES. FOREIGN NATIONALS LIKE THE OTHERS.

WHAT ABOUT THE OTHER 75 BODIES? THEY WERE ALL ISS.
THE REST WERE DARK SOLDIERS. MOST OF THEM TRAINED SINCE ADOLESCENCE IN OFF-SHORE CAMPS.

THE OTHER 75 BODIES WILL NOT CONNECT TO ISS.
"FBI BELIEVES THE ASSAILANTS INFILTRATED AMF SECURITY."

ISS WAS NOT INFILTRATED; I SUSPECT TEAMS EQUIPPED WITH PROSTHETICS AND DRONES NEUTRALIZED MY UNITS AT AMF.
PROSTHETICS EXPLAINS THE HAND IMPRINTS IN THE STEEL CONTAINERS ON THE TOLERANCE AND SECURITY DOOR AT THE ABATTOIR.

WHATEVER KILLED THE ALLIGATORS PUT THE WOMEN TO SLEEP, AND MELTED THOSE WINDOWS.
DRONES COULD HAVE LURED AND REPELLED THE ALLIGATORS AS WELL.

CHAVEZ SENT PEOPLE TO THE FLORIDA CRIME SCENE AND MORTUARY TO FIND AN ALLIGATOR LURE.
THEY ARE ALSO TRYING TO ACCESS KERNS' CLOUD STORAGE.
I CANNOT GUARANTEE THE AMF INVESTIGATION RELEASING ANY IMAGES THROUGH MY OFFICE.
WHAT ABOUT MY IMAGES, EVAN?

CONTACT US WHEN YOU KNOW MORE, JIM.
"HOLANDER IMAGES? UGH–YES, SIR."

WHOOSH!
WHOOSH!
WHUM!
BOTS HAVE BEEN DISTRIBUTING FICTITIOUS IMAGES OF YOU IN MIKE'S BARN FOR THE PAST 12 HOURS. THE PUBLIC WILL ACCEPT REAL IMAGES OF YOU IN PASSING.
WHUM!

OVERSHADOWED BY, MIKE. BLESS YOU, MIKE. FORGIVE ME, BOY.
ROY, YOU NEED TO GET ON AIR ABOUT MIKE BEFORE YOUR IMAGES ARE RELEASED.

OKAY BUT, FELLAS, I THINK MIKE TOLD EL ABOUT AMF.
IF MIKE DID, LADY LIBERTY 2013, AKA EL, WAS MORE THAN JUST A SEXTING PARTNER.

I SUSPECT EL IS AI. MIKE WOULD HAVE DIVULGED HIS AMF OPERATIONS TO AN AI.
SO WHAT IF LADY LIBERTY 2013 IS AI. EL IS REAL! SHE KILLED MIKE!

MIKE COULD HAVE REVEALED CELSIUS TO EL BEFORE HE DIED.
NO, NEUROFEEDBACK FROM HIS CHIP WOULD HAVE PREVENTED IT.

MY PEOPLE IN FLORIDA WERE UNABLE TO RECOVER MIKE'S CHIP.
IF THE CHIP IS THERE CHAVEZ'S PEOPLE MIGHT FIND IT.
THE CHIP IS USELESS WITHOUT MIKE'S DNA IN MIKE'S LIVING BODY.
WOULD HIS CHIP HAVE PREVENTED MIKE FROM TELLING EL ABOUT THE WOMEN HE MURDERED?

NO, IT WOULDN'T. JACK, COULD ONE PERSON HAVE COMMITTED THE WHITE SHARKS MASSACRE?
YES, BUT, SECURITY ON THE TOLERANCE AND AT AMF ABATTOIR WERE SEASONED PROFESSIONALS.

THEIR DEATHS BY ELECTROCUTION AND FEW WEAPONS FIRED INDICATES AN ASSAULT WITH ADVANCED TECHNOLOGY. THAT MEANS RESOURCES.
RESOURCES? YOU MEAN MONEY. BIG MONEY.

THEY WERE ALL ISS EMPLOYEES. THIS COULD BE PAYBACK FOR A MILITARY ACTION ISS TOOK PART IN.
THE FBI IS LOOKING FOR A YACHT. EL COULD WORK FOR SOMEONE RICH MIKE PISSED OFF.

POSSIBLY, ROY. BUT THE DEATH TOLL SUGGESTS RETRIBUTION FOR AN ISS MILITARY ACTION WAS MOST LIKELY THE REASON.
EL WENT OUT OF HER WAY TO GET CLOSE TO MIKE AND KEEP THE WOMEN ALIVE. MIKE'S EXECUTION WAS PERSONAL, DEVON.

I AGREE. MY ISS CASUALTIES AT AMF WERE THE RESULT OF AN ASSAULT ON MIKE.
PERSONAL OR NOT IT TOOK RESOURCES, BIG MONEY TO ASSAULT AMF AND MURDER MIKE.

OBVIOUSLY, MIKE'S DEPRAVITY ATTRACTED SOMEONE OF MEANS' ATTENTION.
SOMEONE OF MEANS.

...ENTICED BY THE SMELL OF SEARING FLESH, MATRON ENJOYS THE COMPANY OF NEW FRIENDS AND PAST SEXUAL ACQUAINTANCES.

JEALOUS AND STILL OBSESSED WITH EL, AKA LADY LIBERTY 2013, MIKE KERNS' FORMER HOUSEMATES, SURVIVORS OF THE WHITE SHARKS MASSACRE, DETAIL THEIR ENCOUNTERS WITH EL TO THE AMF INVESTIGATION. ALL CLUES POINT TO PALANQUIN.

DEVON TRAIT RECEIVES A STERN WARNING AND IS TOLD TO STAY AWAY FROM PEOPLE THAT ARE NOT HIS TYPE.

IT'S A SHOUT OUT TO ALL TRUE HEDONISTS. INFIDELITY RULES! NOBODY'S SPOUSE IS TRUSTWORTHY OR SAFE. MATRON IS IN THE HOUSE...

NEXT EPISODE *"WOKE"*.

orneywines.com

thebookessence.com

thejerusalem14.com

polynlee.com

phascistclowns.com

oldmancupid.com

carltonlewissampson.com

ISBN 978-1-953132-05-5
90000>

9 781953 132055

www.ingramcontent.com/pod-product-compliance
Lightning Source LLC
Chambersburg PA
CBHW041536240626
47164CB00002B/37